Other Novels by Randall Beth Platt

Honor Bright
The Royalscope Fe-As-Ko
The Four Arrows Fe-As-Ko
Out of a Forest Clearing

THE
CORNERSTONE

A Novel by
Randall Beth Platt

CATBIRD PRESS

CATBIRD PRESS
16 Windsor Road, North Haven, CT 06473
800-360-2391; catbird@pipeline.com

Our books are distributed by Independent Publishers Group

This book is a work of fiction, and the characters
and events in it are fictitious.

Library of Congress Cataloging-in-Publication

Platt, Randall Beth, 1948-
The cornerstone: a coming-of-age novel/by Randall Beth Platt.
ISBN 0-945774-40-0 (alk. paper)
1. World War, 1939-1945 — Veterans —
Washington (State) — Fiction.
I. Title
PS3566.L293C67   1998
813'.54—dc21   98-7943

For my sons,
Elkan and Skye Wollenberg
and their gang of wonderful 'hoods'

Also, Rob Wechsler
for his watchful eye and wicked pencil

Lastly, Tom Skerritt
for his faith and patience

These fine men have helped,
each in his own way,
with this creation.

one

The brass, the bullets, the bravado glittered in the noon-day sun. The white perfection of dress uniform, the sanitary gray of the ship, the gently reassuring lapping of the water, all melted into the drone of yet another speech.

Rear Admiral Ian McKenzie, USN looked through his sunglasses at the assembly gathered on the deck before him . . . the spit, the polish, the gold cord, the ladies' hats, the impotent spires of the mothballed battleships in the Bremerton Naval Shipyards. How many times had he been through this protocol? He couldn't begin to remember. Too many years, too many wars clogged the memory. One retirement ceremony was just like another. Speech, salute, speech, salute. Razz, remember, commemorate, decorate, kiss, shake, salute — that's it — golf, write memoirs, die . . . or, as MacArthur preferred, simply fade away.

Whichever.

The air quaked as two jets flew low overhead. A surprise salute? A coincidence perhaps? Or maybe two young smartass pilots from the Whidbey Island Naval Air Station having a looksee at the fleeting pomp as it circumstanced on the decks of the USS *Missouri.*

As the air stilled and the attention of the crowd came back to rest on the podium, McKenzie returned to the moment and realized it was his turn to speak. As all eyes came to rest upon his glorious gold and white, he rose and approached the podium.

Just as surely as the lovely lady *Missouri* underneath him, Rear Admiral Ian McKenzie, age sixty-three, after forty-six years of service to his country, was being ushered out. No Middle Eastern squabble to save either of them this time. It was 1992, and time for them both to move on. She was out. He was out. At long last.

He hadn't prepared a speech. What was there to say? And who out there cared? With Helen and Ian, Jr. dead, what was the point? He took off his sunglasses and looked out over the assembled congregation. Smiling ladies, attentive officers, local luminaries, crackerjacks standing fast around the perimeter of the ship.

He took the easy way out. He smiled and said, "I've been to enough of these to know there's really not much a man can say after forty-six years. Those preceding me here on this dais today have been more than kind. If I had it to do over again, I would. Just as I know ol' Mighty MO would if she could. But things change." He looked at the bunting strung from the once proud cannons, then continued, "But we both received our last orders and so . . . now . . . all there's left to do is. . . " He smiled as best he could, brought his hand up, and saluted.

The chaplain offered a prayer, the Master of Ceremonies ordered the retirement of the colors, and then he said solemnly, "Rear Admiral, United States Navy, departing. . . "

The band started softly playing "Anchors Away" at a

slow cadence as McKenzie walked down off the stage. He stopped and stood in front of his sideboys — eight sailors, four on each side, especially chosen, in bright, perfect crackerjack uniforms. The only movement was their black neckerchiefs, the only sounds the whisper of the band and the flags and bunting snapping in the breeze.

Then, as though to clear the air of such solemnity, Dingding, Dingding, Dingding, Dingding. Eight bells. The sideboys saluted and McKenzie was, once again, a civilian.

Nothing to it.

"Sir? Admiral?" Lt. Lance Harding, McKenzie's adjutant, called in through the office door.

McKenzie, caught smiling down at the last photo taken of his wife and son, snapped his head up and answered, "Come in, Lieutenant." He carefully wrapped the picture in newspaper and added it to the box, nearly full, on his desk. "Just packing up the last few things."

The lieutenant, now in his khakis and looking his thirtyish age, rather than like a shavetail recruit in crackerjacks, appeared in the doorway. "Need help, sir?"

"Almost done, Lance. Thanks. Thanks for everything. Nice ceremony. Went off without a hitch." He took some plaques down from the wall and put them into the box.

The lieutenant placed some letters, faxes, telegrams on the admiral's desk and said, "They keep pouring in. Looks like everyone's sorry to see you go."

McKenzie gave them a cursory look and replied, "Right."

"Oh, and this just came in. It's a confirmation from that Camp Roswell." He handed McKenzie a thin, curled sheet of fax paper.

"Refresh my memory."

"The kids' camp you went to back in forty-four. They're dedicating a new lodge in your name and you said you'd speak at the ceremonies. You agreed last spring, remember, sir?"

"Oh, Christ!" McKenzie moaned as he scanned the letter. "Can you get me out of it?"

"They're expecting you this Thursday, sir, but. . . " the lieutenant said diplomatically, "I could tell them you're not feeling well."

"Yes, all right. Do that." But as the lieutenant started to leave, McKenzie stopped him with, "No, wait, Lance." He paused as he looked at his appointment calendar, clean, white, waiting for adventures to be scribbled in, and said, "Oh sure, why the hell not. It's what, maybe an hour south of here? Nothing better to do. Tell them I'll be there." He turned and looked through his office window at the *Missouri* and whispered absently, "In the cool, cool, cool of the evening . . . tell them I'll be there. . . "

"Sir?" the lieutenant asked.

"I'll *be* there," the admiral replied curtly. How well he and Helen had imitated Crosby and Wyman's crooning.

"Christ," he thought, still looking out the window. "It went so fast . . . "

He called the lieutenant.

"Sir?"

"You tell them anything about my health and I'll see that you wear nothing but that crackerjack getup for the rest of your living days. In fact, I'll see to it you're buried in it!"

The lieutenant smiled in at the admiral and replied, "Aye aye, sir."

That following Thursday afternoon, instead of being greeted with a gush of warm, Puget Sound memories when he walked into Camp Roswell, McKenzie was overcome by an immediate sense of regret. The towering firs, the weathered, hand-carved signs offered no welcome, nor did the smell of the salt air nor the sound of faraway campers at play.

He stopped at the check-in cabin, freshly painted and bright, set his grip down, and wondered what the hell he was doing here. If he was the most notable dignitary the board of directors could dig up among the endless rosters of past campers, then Roswell had hardly inspired greatness.

With the exception of some vocal crows above, no one had noticed his arrival. He briefly considered leaving, then remembered that admirals never retreat, although they could, on occasion, change their mind. But he'd already saluted Lt. Harding and the staff car off. What was he going to do, hitchhike back to Bremerton? Besides, he was here now. Might as well check in, orate, get it over with, and find that condo in Arizona where the air was easier and the widows unrelenting.

Dressed in his cool khakis, McKenzie didn't feel

quite like he fit in with the warm, dark green of the forest. He walked down the path, pulled by the sounds of the waterfront. He stopped at a crossroads of nicely blacktopped pathways. One sign pointed down to 'Registration and Infirmary' and another sign pointed up to 'Ball Field, Rifle Range and Outback.'

A step further down and a ball, tennis it was, zoomed past him. He was barely able to step aside in time to avoid being stepped aside by a large, rampaging dog in pursuit of the missile. The dog, oblivious to rank and uniform, whirled around the admiral, dashed into the bushes, and emerged, grinning, ball in mouth, tail wagging. Just as the admiral instinctively leaned down to extract the ball and propel it and the dog further uphill, there came a shrill whistle from below.

The dog sprang forward in response and dashed off through the bracken. No finely paved roads for he, not when there was a whistle to respond to.

McKenzie smiled and brushed back a slight whisper from his past. He continued his journey toward the waterfront.

A voice, an angry voice, brought him to a halt. "God damn it, Sadler! Get that dog out of here! Last time!"

McKenzie looked down through the trees at a camp counselor, higher echelon no doubt, speaking down to what he could only surmise to be a camper. Barking adamantly at his side was the dog, impatient with such delays. McKenzie stepped closer for a clearer picture of the kid. At first, he was unable to determine its sex, and he had to stifle a chuckle as he inspected the lop-sided haircut . . . closely cut and snowy white above the right ear, shoulder length and blood-red over the left. When he looked past the hair, he finally determined the kid was a boy. Baggy shorts, sloppy ankletop shoes, oversized plaid shirt. "Screw you, Canaday!" the boy hollered back.

"I mean it, Matt!" the man, Canaday, hollered back down to the kid. "Stop encouraging that dog. We have some top brass coming out this week, and I'll be damned if that mutt is going to be peeing on my new rhodies!"

"He's not *my* dog!" Matt screeched.

The dog dropped the tennis ball and watched it roll down the path. Then he retrieved it himself, obediently, as though to taunt the humans barking so needlessly on that bright, wonderful, made-for-ball-chasing summer's day.

Canaday unclipped a walkie-talkie off his belt and spoke into it. McKenzie decided to crouch down until the skirmish below began to cool.

Another counselor type came up to Canaday and Sadler. He handed a rope to Canaday and, with crisp, camp-like efficiency, ran back into the woods.

"Here," Canaday said, handing Sadler the rope. "The soonest the Humane Society can get out here is Saturday morning. Now, take that dog, tie him up outside the service entrance, and go back to your cabin to get ready for dinner. That settles that."

"Tie him up for two days?" Matt asked, horrified. "Like hell I will!"

"Well, we'll take down water and food, of course. But don't think for a minute I'm going to have that filthy mutt hanging around here with all our guests arriving."

With that, Canaday walked briskly back up the path,

leaving the kid, the dog, and the rope behind. McKenzie rose and continued to pick his way down the path.

As he was roping the dog, Matt caught sight of him out of the corner of his eye. "You one of the blow-ups for the dedication crap?"

"Blow-ups?"

"Yeah. You know, mucky-mucks, big-wigs, blow-ups."

"That about sums it up."

"Sweet. Canaday'll wet his pants having a real uniform around here. Wouldn't be surprised if he has you bless his fleet of leaky rowboats."

McKenzie leaned down and pet the dog. "Nice animal."

"Dog's a pest and a fanatic. He's on his way to the pound, dude," Matt said, looking at the admiral through his shock of hair.

The admiral gently lifted the rope off the dog's neck, took the tennis ball out of its slobbery mouth, and tossed it with all his strength out over the bushes until it vanished and, after it, the dog.

McKenzie looked after the dog, smiled, snapped his fingers, and said, "Darn. Got away again." He handed the rope back to the kid and added, "Here, better get rid of this."

Matt smiled at the conflict between the blow-up's rank and actions. He gave a sloppy salute and the admiral returned it, saying, "Carry on, dude." He picked up his grip and continued down the path, thinking that maybe returning to Camp Roswell wasn't such a bad idea after all. And leaving Matt Sadler thinking, no doubt, that just maybe the last two days of camp weren't going to be such a bust after all.

two

The kid retrieved a skateboard from the bushes and skated off down the path at breakneck speed. The camp mutt sped after him, leaping joyously at his side.

McKenzie watched them disappear, then followed the path down.

Turning a steep corner, going through two perfectly neat rows of laurel hedges, he finally saw the cove that sheltered Camp Roswell from the uncertain elements of the Puget Sound. He stepped out of the shade and had to block the sudden brightness of the late-afternoon sun off the water. Another rush of memory.

The old lodge stood before him, almost hidden now among towering pines and taken over by ivy. It looked much smaller and darker. He realized that forty-eight years ago the trees which now reigned over the lodge were only youngsters planted randomly around the structure and, of course, his eyes viewed the world then as enormous, insurmountable, unobtainable. Things weren't so big to him now.

The admiral looked at his watch. 1700 hours. Everyone must be gathering at the campfire pit. At least, he recalled, that's the way they did it back in forty-four . . . songs, antics, announcements by the great fire pit, while three chosen campers laid the fire for the after-dinner revelries. What was it called? Evensong?

Not sure where or when to announce his illuminating presence, McKenzie walked down to the paved service road, set his grip down, and absently tapped his shirt pocket for the oh-so-familiar scrunch of a pack of cigarettes. But instead of cigarettes, he felt a medicine bottle and remembered he hadn't taken his pills that afternoon.

No cigarettes, no ship, no navy, only his memories now for a life-mate. And no welcoming fanfare, either. McKenzie was beginning to feel like he'd arrived at the mortuary a day early for a funeral — all dressed up and no body.

Then, from above, a voice called out, "Admiral McKenzie?"

McKenzie looked up and saw Canaday leaning over the second-story railing of a building. "Oh my gosh," Canaday gushed, "your office said seven and it's only five!"

Then, before McKenzie could utter a syllable, Canaday disappeared off the deck and was almost instantaneously standing next to him. He enthusiastically pumped McKenzie's hand and continued, "I'm so sorry I wasn't there to officially greet you."

"That's all right, Mr. . . . ?"

"Canaday! Ted Canaday. Please call me Ted, Admiral."

"Some nice young man on a skateboard officially greeted me."

"Oh, not Sadler? Tell me it wasn't Sadler. Some

punk with crazy hair? Oh, I'm so sorry, Admiral. Please, don't judge us. . . "

"I'll try not to," he said curtly, cutting him off.

"We try to take a few of these street kids each session. Charity cases, mostly. You know, get 'em off the streets for a few weeks," he continued importantly. He sighed and added, "But, you can't save 'em all. Not even a bright kid like Sadler."

"Service Organization Kid," McKenzie whispered, remembering.

Canaday's face lit at his words and he said, "Yeah, SOKs is what we call 'em. Had 'em in your day too, eh? Lions, Elks, Rotarians, whatever, send 'em out. Most of 'em are, well frankly, Admiral, pains in the rear, but we always have the hope we can turn some punk around. But these days, what with drugs, AIDS, gangs . . . well, it's all we can do sometimes to just cross our fingers and hope."

McKenzie watched him as he spoke. Some people were so impressed by uniform and rank that they gushed incessantly, but McKenzie attributed Canaday's constant babble to the fact that the man was not only hyper, but seemed to take himself very seriously and was anxious for everyone else to do so, too. Was he a frustrated business-man in mail-order camper-chic or an over-grown camper with delusions of grandeur? McKenzie wondered.

"Well, where do you want to start?" Canaday asked, turning 360 degrees and indicating his camp. His eyes came to rest on the new lodge and he said proudly, "Well, there it is: the Ian L. McKenzie Lodge. We moved into it in May. Would have liked to have waited for the dedication, but you've heard that old saying, time waits for. . . ?"

"Yes, I've heard it."

"So, what d'you think?" he asked, indicating the lodge.

McKenzie tried to look impressed and thought he'd done a satisfactory job of conveying this, but before he could go beyond a facial expression, Canaday added with an unwelcomed slap on the back, "Just goes to show you what 2.1 mil can buy. I know that doesn't go far in the Navy, but out here. . . "

"You know, I'm a bit tired," McKenzie said, cutting him off. "Maybe you could just show me my quarters." McKenzie hadn't any more use for Canaday than Canaday probably had for Matt or the mutt. Once again he regretted coming back to Roswell. He was tired and ached for a cigarette, a war, a future. "If you'll just point the way, I'll settle in."

"Of course, of course." He pulled his walkie-talkie from his belt, spoke to someone in a far-off camp hinterland, and then told the admiral with a grand gesture, "Your chariot awaits."

They walked a short distance to where the path widened, and from out of nowhere a golf cart zipped up. A young man jumped out, loaded the admiral's gear into it, and then disappeared as Canaday took the driver's seat.

As they drove, Canaday pointed out various camp amenities, describing them with pride and vigor befitting a man who had a generous board of directors endowing his every wish. He even described things they didn't pass. He gushed on about the infirmary, the gas barbecues, the cafeteria, complete with salad bar and special-needs cuisine, the camp store, the guest speakers, the solar-heated pools.

McKenzie merely nodded and smiled politely.

"And, just the first in what I hope are many surprises is the place we have you staying in, Admiral. We don't keep many records from back in your day, but someone unearthed an old roster that said you stayed in a cabin called Deerslayer."

Deerslayer . . . the word bounced back and forth in the admiral's mind. Deerslayer, what a wonderful word . . . not for its meaning, but for the way it moves the mouth, the mind, the memory.

"Well, it was condemned years ago, but when we heard you were coming back to Roswell, we had it fixed up . . . rewired it. Oh, and we thought plumbing was a nice touch."

Canaday droned on until his walkie-talkie interrupted him. Static on static. He barked importantly back into it, issuing orders, then pulled the cart to a stop. "One problem after another today. You must know how *that* is. Will you excuse me, Admiral?"

Delighted to be rid of him and his obnoxious cheerfulness, McKenzie stepped out of the cart and, extracting his gear, said, "You go on ahead and attend to things. I think I can find it from here."

"Now, how about dinner?"

"My adjutant and I stopped for something on our way out here."

Canaday looked supremely disappointed. "Oh. Well,

we have a special program planned at evensong. All the kids are dying to meet a real Admiral."

"I'll bet."

"Shall we say two-thousand hours? Or is it twenty-hundred hours? I can never remember."

"It's eight o'clock. Sure. And no need to call; I'll find the campfire."

"Just follow the singing," Canaday called out as he backed the cart around and sped off to attend to camp things.

Alone again in the forest, the admiral continued his journey, trying his best to allow his feet to follow their memory to Deerslayer. The closer his instincts took him to the cabin, the more familiar the path, now earth, not pavement, seemed.

A gull called out over the water, and he looked at the cove below, now dazzling in the late-day sun. He rested as he listened for more familiar sounds, then continued up the hill until he saw it . . . Deerslayer, peeking out from under the low-hanging boughs.

A wide smile crossed his face as he approached it. Ancient back when he was a kid, he remembered all the boys had bets on when Deerslayer would topple into the water below. But it had been re-supported by pilings. And the trees had grown to embrace it; from the front it seemed that the large, gnarled roots were holding it lovingly in place.

The porch creaked as though to welcome one last camper into the arms of Deerslayer and to remind him that they both had grown so much older.

He opened the door and was greeted by an odd

aroma of stale salt air, fresh paint, old cedar, and yesterday's Pinesol. Two of the old bunks had been replaced by a bed, desk, dresser, chair, and nightstand.

He set about unpacking his grip, took a pill, and laid down on the bed, exhausted.

His watch peeped him awake at a quarter to eight. The rest had revitalized him. He rose, stretched, and looked out the window. Hordes of campers were making their way toward the campfire. Evensong. Hell, he grumbled. He pulled on a pair of jeans, swapped his starched shirt for a wrinkled plaid, tucked it in, and picked his path down and away from the singing, the campfire, the evensong, and Canaday at its helm.

McKenzie walked down to the waterfront, which was roped off, closed for the day. Rope being merely a shipboard necessity, McKenzie ignored the barrier and strolled out onto the long, beautifully timbered dock.

He pulled a chaise lounge close to the edge and lay down, admiring the beauty of the cove, which as near as he could recall hadn't changed much. The sky was sunset-kissed in purple, the giant evergreens across the cove cast long black shadows on the water, and the sudden coolness of dusk soothed away his weariness. The sounds of children singing at the faraway campfire and the water gently lapping below him combined to lull the admiral into a warming calm. The birds were making their last-effort dashes at the water, and the air was filled with the welcoming scent of salty driftwood burning, creosoted timbers, and low-tide leftovers.

But his serenity was soon stolen by the clunking sounds of wheels along the dock behind him. Without looking, he could visualize the skateboarder ca-chunking down the narrow dock. Obviously, rope barriers meant nothing to the kid either, nor to the dog barking at his side.

Just inches from the end of the dock, the boy coasted to a stop, flipped his board up, caught it, and smiled down at McKenzie.

"Wanna try?" he asked, offering the admiral the board.

"Some other time, Sadler," McKenzie said, keeping his eyes closed, a little disgruntled by the intrusion.

"You can call me Matt."

McKenzie opened his eyes and stared into Matt Sadler's face for a time. Even in the dusky shadows, his eyes glowed bright . . . half boy, half man, full of the devilment of jumping capriciously from one to the other.

"How old are you?" McKenzie finally asked, looking back out over the cove.

"What's it to you?"

"Just curious."

"Fourteen . . . almost."

"They're making them younger these days."

"What younger?"

"SOKs." McKenzie was petting the dog now.

"Shitty Obnoxious Kids?"

McKenzie laughed. Some things didn't change. "Yeah, Shitty Obnoxious Kids."

With sundown as their cue, the night creatures began their serenade along the shores of the cove. That hadn't changed either, McKenzie thought. The singing and laughing was still echoing down off the hillside, accompanied by snaps of protest from the huge campfire. Hopeful embers rose high into the trees, only to extinguish in the coolness of the night and cascade down as black, broken ashes.

Matt sat next to his skateboard and seemed to be enjoying the same night sounds.

"This is more like it," McKenzie said, putting his head back and taking in the beauty of the stillness, the coolness of the air, and the flashy diamonds reflecting off the water.

"More like what?"

"Like it used to be," he answered, almost under his breath.

"Oh yeah," Matt said, "the oooooooolden days. Before they invented the wheel." He spun one of the wheels and its well-oiled wwwwwhirl sounded marvelous against the night sounds.

McKenzie's eyes came to rest on Matt. The hard city punker seemed softer now, watching the water and listening to nature's own evensong.

"Won't Canaday come looking for you?" McKenzie finally asked. "And that mutt? I hear there's an APB out on him."

"Hell, it's *you* Canaday's looking for. He's having a shit-fit wondering where his guest of honor disappeared to."

"Oh. So I didn't see you, you didn't see me."

"Sweet," the kid said. "What about Mutt?"

McKenzie closed his eyes, smiled, and said, "I have an empty bunk."

The singing from within the woods ended, echoed off the bay, and came back again in the familiar refrain of "May God Bless and Keep You."

"You better get back," the admiral said. "Mustn't miss tuck in."

"Oh yeah, man, like I wouldn't clock a Z all night."

The lights throughout the camp flashed on and off, signaling general quarters, and Matt rose, flipped his board up with his toe, caught it expertly, and said, "Later, sailor."

The lights along the waterfront walkway clicked off and, as though suspicious of the sudden darkness, the frogs and crickets ceased their lovesongs for a moment. Then, one by cautious one, overcoming their shyness, they resumed their chants and choruses. McKenzie closed his eyes and listened to the lapping of the water against the pilings below.

Taps was played over the intercom and, in the familiar clarity of the simple yet mournful tune, McKenzie drifted back, allowing himself the luxury of reverie. Remembering the days when a boy, not a recording, offered Taps with all his heart and soul, he looked out over the moonkissed water. He remembered the blinding light the noonday sun had once brought to this cove . . . when the trees weren't so tall, when he could stay forever in the icy Puget Sound water, and when he still had a life ahead to unravel.

Taps ended. Suddenly, the dock wasn't as sweet with creosote or sophisticated in structure, but was long and high and daring. The night was sparkling day, the water rejoiced with the splashing of swimmers, and the air was filled with the laughter of boys wishing to be men, and men pretending to be boys.

It was July. 1944.

three

In the still of the forest sunrise, an old Ford kicked up a cloud of dust as it turned the corner into the Camp Roswell parking lot. It slowed, then came to a halt against a log barrier. Painted on the door were the words 'Bishop Hall - Pierce County, Washington.'

The driver got out, crushed his cigarette into the dust, and then looked into the back seat. He opened the back door with an impatient yank and said, "All right, Mr. Wonderful. Camp Roswell. Haul your butt out."

But Mr. Wonderful, Ian McKenzie, sunk deeper into the seat, his hat pulled down impudently over his eyes, arms crossed defiantly across his chest.

"Look, ace," the driver continued with the season of a man well experienced with the likes of McKenzie, "it's like I told you: boys camp or detention camp, your choice. Too bad you ain't sixteen, then your sorry ass'd go to jail where it belongs!" He looked at his watch and awaited the boy's reply, which was,

"It's *all* bullshit!"

On cue, the driver leaned in and started to yank the boy out with the words, "Oh yeah? I'll show you bullshit!"

Ian, using his small duffel as a breastplate, tried to

struggle, but was no match for the driver. "Knock it off, you son of a bitch!"

The driver grabbed Ian by his jacket and growled, "You punks are all alike. I seen you come and go like shit on a wave. If I had my way, you'd all end up chain gangin' down south. Now move!"

He pushed Ian ahead of him toward a hand-carved sign which said, 'Welcome to Camp Roswell.'

Ian pulled his collar up around his neck and walked down the path arrogantly as he could until the driver pushed him off toward the check-in shed.

Waiting for them there was a tall man leaning casually against the shed, cigarette hanging off a lip. It was barely light out, and the man was nearly hidden in the shadows.

The driver pulled some papers out of his jacket pocket, consulted them, and asked, "You Harry Hyatt?"

The man looked at Ian, giving him a cool up and down, and replied, "Nope. Reckon that don't matter. I'll take this pup off yer hands."

"Well, you can have him! Crazy kid tried to ditch me twice on the way out here." He handed him the papers and said, "Here, sign this."

"He don't look so tough to me," the man replied as he signed the papers.

The driver looked at Ian and said, "Just another two-bit punk. He'll be back at Bishop Hall by September, what do you wanna bet?"

Ian looked off into the woods, his jaw set hard, his breath coming quicker.

"How 'bout it, kid? You wanna lay money on that?" the driver baited, pushing Ian's shoulder.

Ian slapped his hand back and challenged him with a fist, "Keep your hands off me, you. . . "

The driver took a stance to fight, hissing, "You wanna go a round here, kid, huh? Right here?"

But the man caught the driver's fist and said, "Now now, I think I can take things from here. Thanks fer the delivery. If you wanna catch that eight o'clock ferry back to Tacoma, you best start on back."

The driver backed off, snatched the signed papers, and said, "Like I said, September he'll be back." Then to Ian he added, "I'll be waiting for you, punk!"

He walked away, and when his car was out of sight, the man looked at Ian and said, "Y'all gonna stay put while I git yer stuff or am I gonna need to rope you to a tree?"

"It'd take more'n a rope to keep me anyplace I don't wanna be!" Ian said.

"Yeah yeah," the man replied, almost whimsically. "I heard that before." He disappeared into the shed and came back out carrying a thin, folded mattress, a stained pillow, sheets, and a blanket. He looked down at a clipboard, then grinned menacingly down at Ian.

"Eeeon? That ain't no name. That's some kinda era or something. What kinda name's Eeeon?" He held the bedding out to Ian, the cigarette still dangling from his lip.

Ian grabbed the bedding and said, "*My* name. So what're you, the warden?"

"Nope, jest a lowly cabin counselor. Okay, Eeeon

McKenzie, says here yer in cabin number six. Number six is called Deerslayer." He glared down at the kid. The cigarette smoke rising lazily up didn't seem to bother his eyes, eyes of cool alloy, untearing, uncaring. "Well, what'd y'all know? *My* cabin is Deerslayer. Guess this here's yer lucky day. Now, they got these here letters S-O-K next to yer name, son. Now, what y'all reckon that means?" He spoke tauntingly as he showed the boy the clipboard.

Without looking at the roster, Ian replied, "How the hell should I know!"

The counselor scratched his head, looked to the heavens, and said, "Think maybe it means yer stuck out here whether you like it or not."

Ian looked coldly at the counselor and replied confidently, "We'll see about that."

The counselor returned his stare and said, "Reckon we will."

Ian looked down the path and said, "So how do I get to this Doomsayer cabin of yours?"

"Deer-slayer," the counselor corrected, picking up Ian's duffel. "You know, like in James Fenimore Cooper?"

Ian stood his ground, sizing the man, his summer warden.

The counselor noted the heaviness of the duffel. "What the hell you got in here, bricks?" He started to open it.

"Gimme that!"

But the counselor ignored him and opened the duffel, reached in, and brought out three books. He opened one, turned to the first page, and read the inscription:

"To little Ian, for when he can read. Love, Daddy. November 21, 1934." He sniffed dramatically and added, "Ah, I could jest cry."

Ian lunged for the book and hollered, "Give it back, you fucking. . . "

At this, the man reached out and grabbed Ian, jerking him clean off the ground. He held him so close to his face that, while he spoke, Ian could feel the heat from his dangling cigarette.

"Now you listen to me, kid. We got us a summer at close quarters. You wanna reach a understandin' now or later?"

He spoke slowly, deliberately, as though thoroughly enjoying his thick Southern accent.

Ian didn't struggle, but snarled back boldly, "Yeah, if you're such a goddam hotshot, how come you're out here and not fighting the war?"

He drew Ian closer to his face and said, "I done my friggin' fightin', kid. This here's my rest and relaxation. You best see to it I git plenty a' both, cuz you start me another war an' I'll finish that job somebody begun on your throat. We understand each other?"

Ian stared into two hollow green eyes and felt their cold glare clear to the scar on his throat. His heart was pounding so fast, all he could do was nod his head in vague agreement. He saw little point in being sent out from the city's street fights only to be killed by a camp counselor.

An inch at a time, as though gaining control over his anger one relaxing muscle at a time, the counselor let Ian down. Then he growled, "You jest don't know how that happifies me, Eeeon." His voice became velvety and cordial as he picked up the boy's duffel and continued, "Well, come on, young'n, let's git on down to Deerslayer. Don't know why they call it Deerslayer. Prob'ly jest d-lusions. D-lusions a' grandeur. *Rat*slayer's more like it. . . . So tell me about yerself, kid. What side a' the tracks you from, like as though I ain't got a good idea already?"

Although he'd never been to a camp, Ian knew this was hardly the typical camp counselor. A big fish in a small pond, he decided. Tall, thin, dark, dangerous, mysterious. There was a constant glow in his eyes, an intensity that didn't change like his voice and face did. The guy's unbalanced, insane, rabid, Ian concluded. Never take your eyes off of him. Never, not for an instant. Never turn your back. Find the clown in charge of this dump, tell him he's harboring a psycho, and get the hell out of here. Back to Tacoma. Back to the streets.

The counselor pointed out several areas of interest along the path . . . you eat here, piss there, rifle range opens at ten . . . as talkative as though they'd never shared a harsh word. They followed the trail down, then over, and finally up a steep hill to Deerslayer, a rustic cabin, precariously built on a hillside overlooking the cove.

The counselor tossed Ian's grip up on the porch, turned to his charge, and said, "Name's Andrew Jackson Ackerman. Any combination a' those names you wanna call me's fine. Git on up there and meet yer new little playmates, Eeeon."

Ian looked at him defiantly through a shock of

unruly blond hair. He slowly walked past him, coura-geously knocking his arm with a swing of his bedding. He kept on going, up the porch stairs, but was stopped by Ackerman's twangy voice:

"An' don't think yer so all-fired rugged, son. You'll be keepin' some mighty mean company inside that dump. 'Sides, this here's a right proper Methodist camp, and fer havin' fun. So, you havin' fun?" He smiled a broad, sarcastic smile, displaying tobacco-stained teeth. His eyes were almost catlike, and the long, narrow lines of his jaw flexed as he spoke.

"Fuckin' barrels of it," Ian said. He backed up the last step, unsure how Ackerman'd react.

Ackerman looked up at him and asked, "So where's that smile that made ya famous?"

"Screw you!"

Again Ackerman grabbed Ian, yanking him back down the steps. "Smile fer yer Uncle Andy, boy."

Laughter, boys' laughter, coming from within the cabin, trebled Ian's anger. He struggled and kicked, but the wiry man's grip was hard and unyielding.

"Purdy please?" Ackerman asked coyly.

Ian could only bare his teeth in a mock smile of intense hatred. Ackerman released him, threw back his head, and laughed. "Hell, that's one a' the best smiles so far this summer! Yessir, grit an' all!"

He turned, lit another cigarette, and walked back down the path, talking to himself as he walked. Ian was left on the porch to face the Deerslayers alone.

four

To Ian, the whole area around the cabin seemed to grow silent, as though the trees, the waves, the birds were all watching to see what would happen next. In any event, he knew he was being watched by the boys inside. He straightened his shoulders, turned slowly, insolently, and saw four boys staring at him through the cabin window. When their eyes briefly met through fogged-up glass, he felt a familiar dread . . . as though walking into Deerslayer would be like walking into his rival gang's hangout. Or like opening the door at home only to find the man his mother would be entertaining that night, and wondering where the hell he was going to spend the night himself. Now he knew why the man had called the place Ratslayer. It was where all the street rats, the troublemakers, the SOKs were assigned.

He pushed the door open with his foot. He'd seen enough gangster movies to know the importance of making a formidable entrance. Dumping his gear down, he looked around, expecting to meet Bogart, Robinson, Cagney. Make sure they see who's toughest — strike fear — no doubters.

"Who the hell does that jerk think he is?" he demanded, tossing his head vaguely in the direction Ackerman had taken.

"We were wondering the same thing about you," one of the boys said flatly, staring down at him from his upper bunk. He was a strikingly handsome boy, about the same age as Ian. Ian knew this was the one in charge of Deerslayer.

Ian looked around and decided on which bunk to take. He pulled a mattress down off a top bunk with a water view, and placed his own mattress on it.

"Hey, that's *my* bunk!" one of the boys protested. Ian saw he was a scrawny imp, full of lip, one leg permanently embraced by polio.

"Look at you. You can't even climb up here," he said cruelly.

"Oh yeah? Watch this!" In spite of a heavy leg brace, he scrambled up the bunk and threw Ian's mattress onto the floor. Now eye to eye, the small boy challenged Ian: "*My* bunk!"

The good-looking one, the undoubtable leader, jumped down from his bunk and pointed to an empty bunk by the door. "That's your bunk. Where we can all keep an eye on you."

"Why, you all a bunch of fags in here?" Ian asked.

Another boy, hidden in the shadows of his lower bunk, leaped toward Ian and said, "How would you like your face bashed in?"

Ian countered with, "You couldn't even come close, crater-face!"

Crater-face threw the first punch, and they were down and fighting on the cabin floor, being cheered on by the polioed boy and his chubby bunkmate. The leader pulled them apart, saying, "Cut it out, you assholes!

Ackerman'll hear you!" He pulled them apart and stood between them.

"What right's this jerk have coming in here like he owns the goddam place?"

The leader grabbed Crater-face by the shirt and warned him with, "You know what Ackerman said, Soleri: one more fight and you're out of here!"

"I don't care. The kid's a jerk!"

"Look, I'll handle him. You go cool off."

Soleri, Crater-face, pulled his shirt back from Ian's grasp, smoothed it out and, never taking his eyes off of Ian, said, "You and me ain't finished, punk!"

With that he left, slamming the cabin door hard behind him. The boy with polio said down to Ian, "Tony's got a short fuse and nothing between his ears. A real screw-a-roonie."

Then another boy, the tubby one on the lower bunk, added seriously, "He killed a kid in Seattle. I wouldn't mess with him if I were you."

"He did not, Freddy!" the imp challenged. "Stop telling people Tony killed a kid in Seattle! You known goddam good and well it was only Bremerton!"

Ian picked up his mattress, threw it on the empty bunk, and muttered, "A kid like that doesn't have the guts to kill anyone. Best he could hope for is last man in line at a gang shag. Bet him and that Wackerman got lots in common."

The little guy laughed. "Wackerman. That's good, ain't it, Curt? Wackerman."

Curt, the boy in charge, leaned against a bunk and,

still sizing Ian up, said, "Soleri kisses Ackerman's ass. It's enough to make you puke."

"Yeah? Well, they can both kiss mine." Ian busied himself making his bunk, quite aware that his every motion, his every eye-twitch, was being assessed by the three other SOKs.

"So, where you from?" Curt asked.

"Around."

"Where around?"

"Tacoma. What's it to you?"

Freddy poked his head out from his bunk and asked, "What part of Tacoma?"

"The part that doesn't let chubbos in."

This made the little one laugh, and he threw his pillow down at Freddy. "Ha! No chubbos allowed!"

Freddy threw the pillow back with considerable force and said, "Shut up! No gimps allowed either!"

"Chubbo!"

"Gimp!"

Curt ignored the younger rival-pals and asked Ian, "You go to school?"

"On occasion. You?"

"Lincoln."

"Stadium. It's a dump." There were a lot of things he would gladly fight about, but school honor wasn't one of them.

"Just wondered. You got a lousy football team."

"I couldn't give a rat's ass."

"You got a name?"

"McKenzie. Ian."

"Hollenbeck. Curt." He offered his hand and, as

they shook, it was evident by their faces that they were testing each other's strength, hand to hand, eye to eye.

"The baby's Nathanial Roberts. What are you, nine, ten?"

"Ten," he grumbled down to his leader.

"We call him G'Nat," he continued. "He's had polio, but don't let his size fool you. He's tough as nails. The chubbo is Freddy Van Slyke. I think he's pushing twelve. Watch out for him. He'll look you square in the eye and lie like a rug."

"I do not!"

"See? He's doing it again," Curt confirmed.

Ian didn't give them anything more than a casual look of indifference.

"This here's Ackerman's bunk," Curt said, indicating a bunk with tightly made corners and hardly a wrinkle in the blanket. "He keeps it perfect like that, so don't even look at it wrong."

"Ackerman caught Soleri sitting on it, and he came on like gangbusters," G'Nat added. "'Member, Freddy?"

"Yeah, touch that bunk, you die," Freddy concurred.

"Great," Ian said. "You mean, that creep sleeps here, too?"

"Sometimes he does, sometimes he doesn't," Curt said, giving Ian a crooked smile. "You never know with Ackerman. It's his way of keeping us on our toes. Counselors aren't supposed to leave the cabins at night, but. . . "

" . . . Ackerman ain't like the other counselors," G'Nat jumped in.

Freddy concurred, and Curt continued, "Your junk

goes in there." He pointed to a roughly hewn footlocker. "We're not supposed to keep any food in here onaccounta the mice."

"He means rats. We got rats *this* big," Freddy the Liar said seriously, holding his hands four feet apart.

"He's lying. Take everything he says and cut it in half," Curt advised.

"Yeah, the rats are only this big," G'Nat said, holding his hands a mere two feet apart.

"That's right," Curt said, smiling at his younger worshipers. The kid had passed through puberty without a hitch, Ian thought. Clear complexion, thick wavy hair, unwavering voice. Girls must go wild for this stud, he concluded.

Ian tossed his belongings into the footlocker and Curt pulled out a sweatshirt that had 'Stadium Football' on the front. "Like I said, you got a lousy football team." Ian grabbed the shirt back, tossed it, wadded up, into the locker, and lay down on his bunk.

"So, what're you in for?" Curt asked.

"My health," Ian replied blandly, looking up at the rusty criss-crosses of wire holding the sagging upper bunk.

"No, he means what'd you do? If you're in Deerslayer, you're a SOK. You a J.D. or just a problem child?" Freddy persisted.

"I passed J.D. First Class when you were still shittin' in your pants," Ian mumbled.

"You might as well fess up, wise guy," Freddy said plainly, parentally. "You don't pull Deerslayer time unless you're at least an arsonist."

G'Nat took exception and piped in with, "Nunt-uh, you guys're here 'cause you got *caught* screwing up. I'm here 'cause I *ain't* been caught. Yet."

Ian tired of the interrogation and, looking at Curt, asked, "So, what'd you get caught doing?"

Curt replied, "All you gotta know is *I'm* the one in charge here."

Ian turned his back on the rest. "We'll see."

Curt kicked him in his back and repeated, "You got that, kid? I said I'm in charge!"

Having never in his life turned his back without proper protection, Ian whirled around, seized Curt by the shirt, pulled him down forcefully to his knees, snapped a switchblade open, and held it against his throat.

"And I said, We'll see."

Freddy and G'Nat's eyes widened with shock. Impressed shock. Curt smiled weakly and held up his hands. Ian released him, and Curt stood up, stepped back, stared down.

Then, with perfect timing, the camp intercom switched on and a voice cascaded out saying, "May I have your attention, please? We would like to welcome the new boy who just arrived at camp. Now, I want all you old-timers to make the new-timer welcome. It's almost seven, men. Time for Big Dipper!"

The timing and the content of the message brought a smile to Ian's face and an end to the tension in Deerslayer. He returned the blade to its hiding place and asked, "Okay old-timers. What the hell's Big Dipper?"

"Curt's schwantz!" Freddy said, giggling with G'Nat.

"Knock it off, you gimps!" Curt demanded. Then he

looked at Ian and said, "Big Dipper is the morning swim. Rain or shine. Another crappy Roswell tradition. Mandatory."

"Lucky me, I forgot my swimsuit," Ian said, fluffing his pillow.

"Yeah, lucky you," Curt continued, "'cause we don't wear 'em out here."

G'Nat and Freddy exchanged glances, smiled, and began to strip. Curt casually, almost benevolently, helped G'Nat with his leg brace.

"If you don't show up for Big Dipper, it's three demerits for the whole cabin, wise-guy," Freddy said, wrapping a towel around his generous waist.

"So, what if I can't swim?" Ian said, playing now with his switchblade.

"You drown," Curt answered. "Look, McKenzie, you better get one thing straight right here: Don't go lousing things up for the rest of us. You better show up or Ackerman'll kick your butt here to sundown."

"Let him try," Ian answered.

The four towel-enshrined SOKs left. Once outside the cabin, they quietly and quickly walked toward the back where their swimsuits hung on a line. They snatched them off, pulled them on and, G'Nat hitching a ride on Curt's back, took a side trail down to the waterfront to await Ian's entrance and official induction into Camp Roswell.

five

The shoreline was still cool; the sun had yet to reach it. The towering pines swayed gently, as though chuckling in anticipation.

Ian, towel around his waist, stepped carefully out onto the porch. He could hear the boys splashing and laughing down below, and he considered taking off. He flashed on the circumstances that had landed him here, in Camp Roswell. He considered his past and looked down at his future. With a limp frown of resignation, he leaped down off the porch, pell-melled down the path, ripped the towel off, charged the water, and dove into the icy wavelets. It wasn't until he came back up that he noticed he was the only one without a swimsuit.

The campers were lining the waterfront, laughing and pointing and, in the middle of this gathering, Curt was holding up Ian's shed towel and laughing the hardest. Most new initiates wised up to the stunt before entering the water.

Ian couldn't swear or hit or run while treading water. He did the only thing he could under the circumstances: he dove and swam underwater toward the delectable seduction of a nearby buoyed motorboat.

Curt searched for Ian along the waterfront, muttering under his breath. Freddy approached him and asked,

"Hey, where'd he go? Maybe he wasn't lying when he said he can't swim."

"He can swim all right," Curt mumbled. "He's out there screwing around. He can't take a joke, that's all. He's a jerk."

Ian surfaced on the other side of the boat. The sun had crested the treetops, and it offered shade and protection from the eyes of the laughing campers back toward shore. He rested a few moments, then pulled himself up just far enough to spy on the shore. Then, with an easy push, he slipped over the side and into the boat, keeping low.

It was a Chris Craft, brand new. He rummaged around it, marveling at the tuck-and-roll upholstery, the shiny, well-rubbed wood, and the warm, golden brass. He opened the side hatches, pulled out various things, and nearly yelped for his good fortune when he pulled out a pair of baggy, ugly but, what-the-hell, swimming trunks.

He slipped them on and lay for a few moments between the seats, planning his next move. He looked up under the console and spied a key hanging down, hidden from most would-be vandals, but quite visible to the one now enjoying the boat's concealing comforts. He slipped it off its hiding place and tried it in the ignition. A mere formality; he knew it'd fit. He popped his head up slightly to ensure his position and replaced the key. Then, thanking the new-found SOK gods, he slipped back over the side of the boat and began to stroke back to shore.

G'Nat was the first to notice Ian's strong stroke as he approached. "Hey, Hollenbeck, look who's coming."

Curt's face filled with an evil smile. "Gimme that towel, G'Nat," he commanded.

He took the towel, wet the end, rolled it, tightened it, and stood waiting.

"Mur-der! This I gotta see!" G'Nat said, limping over to Freddy to get his attention. "Watch this."

Ian stopped when he could touch bottom. He stood, eying his foe and his towel. He noticed Ackerman back among the trees, standing, smoking, watching. Other boys had been alerted and were lining the beach, awaiting the new kid's reemergence into camp.

Ian walked slowly, a smile beginning to form on his face. Curt returned the smile and held his weapon. Ian's shoulders emerged, then his chest. He stopped and adjusted the baggy trunks before walking further.

"Come on out, McKenzie. Got a nice towel waiting for you."

Ian kept his eyes on Curt as he continued out of the water. He longed for a camera to record for all time the expression on Curt's face as he beheld the trunks.

Ackerman could be heard laughing in the distance, but Ian continued toward Curt, determined to have it out.

Ian stepped to Curt, adjusted his trunks, took the towel, and said, "Thanks for the towel, kid."

"How'd he do that?" Freddy exclaimed.

Curt, angry and foiled once again, whirled Ian around and hollered, "You're a goddam asshole, McKenzie!"

Ian picked up G'Nat's leg brace and threw it to him before replying to Curt, matter-of-factly, "And you're a son of a bitch."

The other campers were soon surrounding them, egging them on, vicariously anticipating the SOKs having it out. But Ackerman was on them now, coolly, calmly. He looked at his SOKs and said, "That's it. Fun's over. Y'all git on back to the cabin."

Ian and Curt glared at each other a moment longer, each determined to finish it later . . . alone, no witnesses. Street rules.

Ian put his towel around his neck and started to leave with the others, but Ackerman pulled him back.

"'Cept you."

"What?"

"Y'all wanna compare chips, boy?" he asked, lighting a cigarette and watching the smoke drift by.

"What the hell's that supposed to mean?" Ian asked back defiantly.

"Bet the chip on my shoulder's bigger'n yers," Ackerman drawled. "'Course, mine's been knocked off so many times I reckon the chip's got chips." He leaned up against a stack of overturned rowboats and looked out over the cove.

"Huh?" Ian asked impatiently, wondering if yet another chip-lecture was brewing. If he had a nickel for every time someone had talked to him about shoulders and chips and attitude, then he sure as hell could have bought his way out of Tacoma.

"Chips is okay, in their place," Ackerman continued, "providin' you know how to wear 'em. They's kinda like wearin' spats. Not every man can pull it off." He looked peacefully at the boy and pulled out his pack of cigarettes. "Smoke?"

Ian ignored the offer and pointed up the hill. "*He's* the one with a chip on his shoulder!"

"Reckon ol' Curt cain't wear spats," Ackerman said, holding up the cigarettes again. "You sure you don't wanna gasper? Might settle yer nerves some."

"Say, just what kind of a set-up is this, Ackerman?" Ian asked boldly, but keeping his distance. At least, he figured, at the rate this man smoked, he could easily out-run him if it came to that. "They told us no smoking out here."

"Now that there's yer basic double standard, boy. Why, at yer age you must be acquainted with several a' those by now." He leaned back, took a long drag on his cigarette, and looked up at the trees overhead.

Ian took a step closer. "What happens when you get caught?"

"When *I* get caught, nothin'. When *you* get caught. . . " He paused and then shook his head hope-lessly, as though closing his eyes on the world's greatest atrocity. "Well . . . it ain't a purdy sight."

"What?" Ian's curiosity was aroused. "Send you home with a nasty note pinned to your jacket?"

Ackerman's long, thin face crinkled with what appeared to be a pained smile. "Hell no, son! That's what they do if you *don't* git caught! Yer a SOK, remember. They's expectin' big things outa you. All us in Deerslayer is SOKs, one way or t'other. Now Harry Hyatt, he's the boss of this outfit, he's got his eyes on us all the time. It jest makes me feel awful to think a' disappointin' him."

Ian studied Ackerman, who was enjoying his cigarette as though it were his last. He was younger than he'd first thought, Ian decided. Twenty-five, thirty maybe. Hard to tell.

"So, how is it *you're* here?" Ian finally asked. "Somehow I get the feeling this isn't your life calling."

"Ain't got me a life callin'," he replied simply, looking back at Ian and dragging on his cigarette.

"So you end up a camp counselor . . . this must be where all the misfits are quarantined." No sooner was the remark out of his mouth than Ian realized maybe he shouldn't have let it out.

But instead of an outburst, Ackerman simply nodded and said, "Meybe so. Meybe so." His face was suddenly somber, almost tragic.

Ian swished his towel over his shoulder. He longed for the coolness of the cove and people less complicated than SOKs. He stepped closer to the water. "I'm going for a swim."

"Glad to see y'all got yer pants on this time," Ackerman called down to Ian as the newest SOK gingerly picked his barefoot way along the waterfront.

Ian was knee deep in water when he turned and asked Ackerman, "This Hyatt guy, the honcho, that his boat?"

Ackerman flicked his cigarette — hissss — into the water and answered, "Yup. And those're his shorts you got on." He turned and lumbered up toward the cabin, adding, "Reckon you don't wanna ferget about breakfast, boy."

Ian dove into the water, enjoying the stillness, the solitude.

*   *   *

He heard him before he saw him, cantering down the path from the lodge, but he knew at once it must be the commander of the works. The swimmer popped his head out of the water and watched him approach. He laughed as the man slowed down to an urgent walk-run in response to the NO RUNNING! sign on the dock. He was a plump little fellow who moved quite well in spite of himself. Ian began rehearsing his lines, but kept paddling about in no great urgency.

"You there!" Harry Hyatt shouted, standing with his hands on his hips. "Come out of that water, son!"

Ian's first impression was that Hyatt was a victim of too much responsibility and too much heat. His round face seemed like red clay that had been left out in the sun too long. The result was a terra-cotta complexion and sourful eyes that sagged down to a button nose which, in turn, weighed heavily upon a down-turned mouth. His chest seemed to have melted down and got caught by his belt where it had hardened and no doubt become the butt of endless jokes. He was the saddest looking man Ian had ever seen.

Ian swam toward the dock, shooting spouts of salt water as he eased along. He looked up innocently and gurgled, "You talking to me?"

"Indeed I am, young man! Come out of there at once! Big Dipper is over. This waterfront is closed. Don't you see that rope?" He pointed over to the rope which cordoned off the waterfront.

"No, sir," he lied.

"You're the new SOK, aren't you?" Hyatt demanded.

Tiring of the label, Ian looked Hyatt in the eyes and said, "Ever think of just branding us right here?" He pointed to his forehead.

"Well, since this is your first day, I can't expect you to know the schedule and the rules. But when you see that rope across the waterfront area, this place is off limits, mister." As he spoke, his voice softened. "Now, I'm Harry Hyatt, Camp Director. And you are?"

Despite his pompous appearance, Ian knew this was no tough guy. A soft-centered piece of rock candy. Either too old for active duty or too fallible to be a leader of men, or maybe just too large for general-issue uniforms. No doubt the command of this post was the highest rank he could attain in war, perhaps in life.

Ian offered a dripping salute and answered, "Ian McKenzie, SOK First Class, reporting for duty, *sir!*"

"Now now," Hyatt said, his voice smooth and foster-fatherish, "no rank, no saluting at Camp Roswell, son. Just follow a few simple rules and I promise you'll have the time of your life. Now, get on up to your cabin. Breakfast at 0800 hours." He tried to smile as much as his dourful face would let him, then scurried back up the dock and disappeared into the woods.

Ian felt his stomach begin to growl and wondered what kind of food the place offered. He climbed out of the water, wrapped his towel around his waist, and walked toward Deerslayer.

Halfway up, Ian ran into Ackerman, who was sitting on a log whittling on a stick and smoking. Without looking up, Ackerman asked, "So, what'd you think a' ol' Hyatt?"

Ian stopped. "He's manageable," Ian answered tentatively.

"I reckon ol' Harry'd rather be in the middle of the war'n here," he explained.

"So who wouldn't!"

Ackerman kept whittling, but looked up through the smoke at Ian, his green eyes not about to reveal a thing.

Ian stared back, then retreated further uphill toward Deerslayer.

"That guy's crazy," he mumbled to himself as he approached the cabin. "Certifiably, one-hundred percent, without the shadow of a doubt, cuckoo!"

"Who is?" Freddy asked.

Ian stopped and found himself looking down at his chubby cabin mate, sitting on the bottom step.

"Wackerman, that's who!" Ian said.

"You're the one talking to himself," Freddy remarked logically. He'd yet to put on his shirt, making him appear even more roly-poly. His fair skin was blotchy from the cold water and his hair was matted to his round face. Yet he seemed to be satisfied and even comfortable within his rotundity, in spite of the unbearable teasing fat kids must endure.

"Yeah. Well, all the same," Ian continued, "he's missing a few marbles."

"Aw, give him a break. He can't help it," Freddy said.

"Who you talking about?" Curt asked from out of the cabin window.

"Andy Ackerman. Who else?" Freddy replied, either out of patience or out of breath as he jumped the steps back into the cabin.

"Look, there's something you might as well know about Ackerman," G'Nat said, his face appearing next to Curt's.

"What, that he's wacko?"

"He's not wacko!" G'Nat said defensively as he stuck his head out the window.

"Then you are for thinking he ain't!" Ian accused.

Curt turned to G'Nat and said, "Shut up, twerp. Let the bigshot find out for himself."

"Screw you, Curt. I'll tell him if I want to." There was a shuffling sound from inside, following by a loud thunk on the floor, then little G'Nat appeared in the doorway, rubbing an elbow. He looked down at Ian and announced importantly, "Ackerman's from Madigan."

"Madigan Hospital? So big deal. What of it?"

"Well, they sent this guy out for . . . well, I guess it's some kinda therapy."

"Therapy?" Ian asked.

"Yeah, like I used to get. Only he gets it in his head, not his leg," G'Nat replied.

"Then I was right! He *is* a mental case!" Ian said flatly.

"Look, Ackerman's in the Navy," Freddy whispered from inside the cabin.

"Let's see now, you're the one who lies, right?" Ian said.

"Fine, don't believe me," Freddy bit back. "No skin off my nose."

"He ain't lying," G'Nat interrupted. "Ackerman's shell shocked. But there's a difference between being shell shocked and plain out wack-a-roony."

"Yeah, and I bet he told you he was a big hero or something," Ian continued, toweling off his hair and walking into the cabin.

"Matter of fact, he doesn't know we know," Curt said as Ian started to pull his pants on. "I happened to overhear some of the other counselors talking about it. None of us are supposed to know. What would your momma say if she thought her sweet baby boy had a counselor who was a little. . . "

"Shell shocked," G'Nat finished for him.

"She'd say he was just her type," Ian said with a crooked smile, pulling his Stadium Football sweatshirt over an old plaid shirt.

Tony Soleri, absent from Big Dipper, appeared in the doorway.

"You still here?" he asked Ian.

"Yeah, but now that you are, I think I need some fresh air," Ian countered, pulling his cap down and walking toward the door.

Curt pulled him back as he passed his bunk and said, "Look, I'm warning you, McKenzie, Ackerman can be real hot and cold. He doesn't like anyone upsetting the natural order of things."

"Then they should have left me the hell in Tacoma," Ian returned, looking at Soleri. He left and, realizing he didn't know where the dining hall was, walked around the back of the cabin and sat down on a tree stump, close to the open back window.

"Forget it, Hollenbeck! I'll take care of that creep my own way," he could hear Soleri say.

"And I'm telling you to let it ride or you'll get us all kicked out of here!" Curt shot back.

"So what? I'm tired of all this camp shit anyway!"

Then G'Nat's small, determined voice, "Well, maybe we're not, Soleri, so don't go screwing it up for the rest of us!"

"Yeah, moiderlate him back in town," Freddy added in an attempt at a Bronx accent.

Then Tony Soleri said lowly, "I want him *out* of here!"

Followed by Curt's commanding voice of cool, "Sure, Tony, so do I. But all in good time. Look, I got some ideas. But for now, you're going to play this my way. Got that?"

No answer.

"Got that?"

"Yeah yeah, I got it!"

"All right. Let's go eat," Curt ordered.

Ian dashed off into the woods and hid until the other SOKs were well ahead of him.

six

Ian followed the SOKs down to a treed hillside overlooking the cove. The dining hall was a large, two-storied, well-windowed affair, with a covered deck that spilled out from several sets of French doors.

The noise that escaped the dining hall was the noise of boisterous energy, of youth and well-earned hunger, of plans for the day, of war news that leaked in over the radio or through letters from home, of easy bantering, of dishes clamoring.

The SOKs instinctively held back, entering last, as an entity rather than as individuals. But if the SOKs were noticed at all, it was with intentional indifference, for SOKs were SOKs, not real campers, not chosen companions, not preferred company for their parents' Methodist offspring. But after what had happened down at the waterfront, this was a special occasion.

Ian stood in the doorway now, and neither the knotty pine, the smell of pancakes, his grumbling hunger, nor even his damn curiosity could pull him inside.

Ackerman, silently and as from nowhere, appeared directly behind him and said, low and easy, "Take a tray, boy. Put a smile on yer face. Yer bein' watched."

Ian didn't budge, but looked around arrogantly, and indeed he was being singled out for notice.

"Why, these boys is jest cupcakes compared to yer
regular bunch," Ackerman added. Still, Ian didn't move.
"Ain't they?" Ackerman whispered, giving Ian a slight
shove.

"Yeah, sure," Ian agreed as he took a step on his
own. He noticed no one was eating.

Ackerman followed his glance and said, "They's
waitin' fer you, Eeeon."

He took a tray and walked toward the serving
counter, held it up against the weight of pancakes, then
started walking toward the farthest corner of the dining
hall.

"Nope. Over here, Eeeon," Ackerman said, pulling
Ian's sleeve. "Yer sittin' here with yer little friends. And
don't eat till yer told to."

Ian glared daringly at the other SOKs, sat, then took
the cap off his pint of milk and raised it to chug. Freddy
elbowed him and indicated the counselors' table. A
silence grew over the room as Hyatt stood and hit a note
on the piano not far from his chair. On this cue, the
boys stood and placed their arms around each other's
shoulders. Ian remained seated, drinking his milk. Then
to the tune of "Oh Christmas Tree" the congregation
sang:

> We thank thee, Lord,
> For food this day,
> We thank thee, Lord,
> And so we pray
> For peace on earth,
> Eternal good,
> We thank thee, Lord,
> For brotherhood.

Ian watched incredulously as the corny prayer-song poured out, even from the lips of his fellow SOKs. He finished chugging his milk before the prayer ended, then smiled sarcastically as the others held the last long note: ". . . hooooooood."

"You may all be seated," Hyatt said. "I would like to remind you boys that nothing is to be consumed until the counselors begin . . . most especially, no one eats during our prayer of thanks which is offered standing, arm in arm, and with the respect any prayer of thanksgiving deserves."

He was looking directly at Ian, who simply offered back a milk-mustachioed smile, then a burp. He then offered his empty milk bottle up and said, "I give thanks."

Hyatt glared first at Ian, then at Ackerman. Ackerman simply started to cut his pancakes and held the first bite up, waiting along with the rest of the campers for Hyatt to begin.

Hyatt looked around, then snapped out his napkin and took the first bite, whereupon a general frenzy of ravenous boys commenced.

Ian kept silent as he ate, glancing occasionally across the table at Soleri, who silently challenged him by giving him an angry stare and popping him the finger.

Finally, the hall began to empty, and when the counselors had left, G'Nat said, "Hey, you guys hear the one about the priest and the prostitute?"

"No, but I heard the one about the Jap and the Wop," Ian responded, grinning at Soleri.

At that, Soleri reached over and knocked the syrup pitcher over. The syrup swamped over Ian's plate. Ian pushed his chair back as the syrup slinked to the floor. Those at the SOK table, those still left in the dining hall, watched and waited for Ian's next move.

"Whoops," Tony said.

Ian knew he was being set up, but wasn't about to take the first shot. He said, "You mean, wops. . . "

Tony leaped across the table, and Ian rose, then stepped aside and waited for Tony's flailing arms. Such an amateur, he thought. Tony fell into another table, sending the contents sprawling. He picked up a fork and started to circle Ian.

Ian had his switchblade out and ready when he saw Hyatt and Ackerman come running back in. Tony stopped and Ian said, "Ah, you're nothing but a yard dog. Ain't worth the trouble." He closed the knife and tossed it to the floor.

Curt saw it, toed it closer to him, and dropped his napkin on it, hiding it from the adults.

Hyatt grabbed Soleri by the arm and shouted, "Stop it now, both of you! I want everyone out of here except you SOKs! Get to work cleaning this mess up! Soleri, you're coming with me."

"But I didn't. . . " he started. Hyatt hooked his arm tighter and started for the door. As he passed Ackerman he said sternly, "This has got to stop! I want you and that boy in my office as soon as this mess is cleaned up! Come on, son."

Ackerman took Ian by the arm, squeezed tight, and snarled, "What'd I tell you 'bout starting wars, Eeeon?"

"Hey, let up, Andy," Curt broke in. "That kid

didn't start it, Tony did." He looked to G'Nat and Freddy for corroboration.

"That's right, Andy," G'Nat said innocently.

"Yup, sure as I ate thirty-six pancakes, it's true," Freddy concurred, causing G'Nat to look toward the heavens.

"That so?" Ackerman asked Ian.

"Soleri's been asking for it since I got here."

Ackerman released him, then said, "All right, y'all heard Hyatt. Clean this shit up." He went out onto the deck, lit a cigarette, and looked out over the cove.

Heads low, cleaning food off the floor, Ian asked Curt, "All right, what gives? Why'd you do it?"

"I want Soleri out," Curt replied, his face stone cold.

"Why?"

"'Cause he was gonna get us all kicked out," he stated. He noticed Ian was looking around the floor and, holding the switchblade up, Curt asked, "This what you're looking for, McKenzie?"

"You handing it over to Ackerman?"

"I'd be a fool to hand it back over to you. So why don't I just hang onto it for a while. Then, if I want *you* out, it'll be easy as flicking a switch." He switched the blade open, then closed it artfully and slipped it into his shirt pocket. "Like I said, *I'm* in charge." With that he picked up a trayful of dishes and walked toward the kitchen.

Ian smiled confidently as he passed and said, "And I said, we'll see."

*   *   *

After the room was clean, the floor swept, the tables cleaned, the benches stacked, Ackerman stepped back in and called, "Eeeon," and then went out and strolled the path. Ian took his apron off and followed him, with belligerent steps. Ackerman stopped in front of a log building with the carved sign 'Administration' over the front door. He lit a cigarette and looked casually at his watch.

"By my calculations, y'all ain't even been here three hours."

"That's three hours too long."

"Git inside," he said, his voice low and troubling. He opened the screen door and Ian shouldered through.

Hyatt looked up from his cluttered desk and said, "Sit down, Andy. You too, son. Pull up a chair."

"He can stand," Andy said. He took the leather chair, folded his legs, and knocked the cigarette ashes into his pants' cuff.

"Very well," Hyatt began. "Now, Andy, this boy has only been here a few hours. . . "

"Three. I tol' him that."

"And yet there's been two altercations already."

"Two?" Ackerman asked, looking at Ian.

"Yes," Hyatt explained, "your new boy and I had a little run in after Big Dipper this morning. But I thought we'd reached an understanding."

Ian looked away, clearly not interested.

"Where's Soleri?" Ackerman asked.

"Well, I called his case worker and we've agreed it's in everyone's best interest if he left Camp Roswell. We all agreed he needs something more than what we have to offer."

"He needs about ten minutes on *my* turf, that's what the punk needs!" Ian broke in.

Ackerman pointed his long, thin finger and his cigarette at him, and warned, "Y'all speak when yer spoken to, boy!"

Hyatt shifted his considerable weight, and Ian could see he was not comfortable with this side of camp administration. No doubt he'd rather be out on his Chris, fishing, having a beer, or fighting in the backwaters of the Pacific — hell, who wouldn't!

"So, what about *him*?" Ackerman asked.

Hyatt looked sadly down at Ian's file on his desk and flipped through the pages. "I don't know, Andy. What would you do?" He handed the file to Ackerman, who simply placed it back on the desk unopened.

"I reckon you oughta leave him fer me to handle."

"I let you handle Tony Soleri."

He nodded ever so slightly toward Ian and replied, "This one's different."

Hyatt looked at Ian, a kindness, a struggle of good intention in his eyes. "Maybe you and I best discuss this alone, Andy."

Ian turned to leave. Finally! Escape!

"Stay where you are, boy," Ackerman warned. "You ain't been dismissed."

"He said he wanted me out of here and that's okay by me!"

"And I said you ain't been dismissed." He turned to Hyatt, adjusted his tone, and added, "Anything you got to say 'bout him or me or my other SOKs you can say right now. It don't matter what he hears."

"All right, Andy, since you insist." He took a fishing lure off his desk and fingered it while he spoke. "Andy, I know this summer hasn't been easy for you. You came out here in good faith that you would get some rest and I'm sure if you knew you'd end up dealing with a cabin full of delinquents, maybe you wouldn't have. . . "

"Spare me the maybe's. Git on with what you need to say."

"Andy, I've had it up to here with your gang of Dead End Kids. There's been nothing but one problem after another. You know, I used to think there wasn't anything wrong with any boy that a good camping experience couldn't fix. I don't know, but this summer has been enough to change my mind. Maybe I was wrong to have saddled you with the SOKs. Now, I know the war is to blame — manpower shortages, troubled kids, fathers gone, mothers in the factories. . . "

He paused, looked at Ian, then indicated a list on his desk. "Look, thirty-six boys on the waiting list. I just can't handle them. Don't have the manpower. I don't have the facility. Here's another example." He picked up a paper and read, "The Board sends its regrets that they will be unable to build the well-needed and long-deserved dining lodge fireplace and chimney this summer." He tossed the paper down and ran a hankie over his face. Ian wondered if he was near tears.

"No manpower," he went on. "Six years I've been waiting for that thing to be built and now, no manpower. Heck, Andy, even my maintenance man's someplace in the Pacific. Yet they want me to take on thirty-six more boys."

Ackerman snuffed out his cigarette on the floor and tidily placed the butt into his shirt pocket. Then he said, "All that ain't got nothin' to do with me an' that kid."

"One week, Andy," Hyatt continued, as though the episode about the phantom fireplace had given him the strength to make a decision. "One week to straighten him around. I hate to be hardshelled about this, but I just have to be."

"Yer dismissed, boy. Wait fer me up at Deerslayer," Ackerman ordered with a motion of his head.

Ian felt as though he'd been holding his breath the entire time. He walked up the path, reconsidered, and then went back to the Admin Hall door; eavesdropping was a major calling to him.

He heard Ackerman saying, "You done the right thing, Harry."

"I mean it, Andy. One week with McKenzie."

"No, I mean you done the right thing givin' me the SOKs."

Ian heard Ackerman's chair scoot back and he quickly darted behind a hedge. Instead of heading toward Deerslayer, Ackerman walked casually back down to the dining hall. Ian watched as Ackerman paused on the grass and looked up the two-storied side of the building, lit another cigarette, then 'thumbed' the building as an artist might 'thumb' his subject for proportion and balance. Then, with a lanky, resolved walk, he took the path back into the Admin Hall, letting the screen door slam behind him. Ian vanished into the woods.

seven

On the trail toward Deerslayer, Ian paused at the fork with signs that advised 'Baseball Field' and 'Parking Lot.' He looked down at the cove and considered his next move. Where the hell was he, anyway? Was there even any civilization around, any cars on the road to hitch a ride with? And the ferry, how much did that cost? He wanted out, but he understood the word 'stuck' when it slapped him in the face. He also comforted himself with the words, 'Just for now,' and continued on the trail toward Deerslayer.

Curt was combing his hair, and G'Nat and Freddy were side by side, sharing a dog-eared copy of *God's Little Acre*. No one greeted him, so Ian lay down on his bunk and stared at the mattress above.

Finally, G'Nat, marking his place in the book, looked over and asked, "You kicked out?"

To which Freddy added, "If you are, you set a new record . . . one whole half of one whole morning."

G'Nat got up, limped to his footlocker, pulled out a bundle wrapped in a napkin, and offered it to Ian. "What's this?" he asked, taking it.

"I swiped a coupla muffins from the kitchen while we were cleaning up. It's a long ride back to Tacoma. Thought you'd get hungry."

"I'm staying here. For now."

"Aw, take 'em anyhow."

Unsure of how to thank such a simple, sincere offering, Ian just said, "Thanks, twerp."

"And I been thinking," G'Nat added, a flow of youthful hero worship budding in his eyes. "That top bunk's a pain in the ass, up and down all the time. Wanna trade?"

"Yeah. Sure. Thanks."

Curt, finally happy with his hair, put the brush down and looked at Ian in the mirror's reflection. "So where's Soleri?"

"You got your wish, Bright Boy. They ratted him out."

"Told ya," Freddy said to G'Nat.

Curt smiled confidently, handsomely, back into the mirror and said, "All in a day's work."

Ackerman's footsteps were heard on the steps, and the door gently swung open. "0900. Inspection."

Not sure what this meant, Ian looked to the others' response, but none of the boys stopped what they were doing. No standing at attention, no moaning, nothing.

The counselor strolled over to the younger boys, picked up the book on G'Nat's lap, and inspected it. "Yup, this here's *God's Little Acre* all right. Now don't none a' you go droolin' on the good parts, y'hear? I want that book back in good condition." Then he walked over to the footlockers and opened each lid. Peering inside each, he nodded approvingly. "Looks mighty fine, men. Y'all only got one beer left, Curt, but ya done a mighty good, patriotic job a' rationin', boy."

He reached into Freddy's box, pulled out a large tin container, and gently rattled it. "Now that's usin' yer head, Freddy. Ain't no rat alive can git yer marshmellers now." He tossed it to Freddy, who opened it and rationed marshmallows to himself, G'Nat, and Curt.

Then Ackerman reached into Ian's box and pulled out the switchblade, still wrapped in the camp napkin. Ian glared at Curt, and the others held their breath. Another set-up, Ian thought, damning himself for not seeing it coming.

Ackerman held the knife up to the light of the window and flicked it open, his eyes glowing. A weapon in Ackerman's hand disturbed them all. Ackerman turned to Ian, eased the blade back into the shaft, and tossed the knife to him.

"Needs oilin'. An' we got us a rule against sech implements a' war out here to camp."

Ian took the knife, slipped it under his pillow, and said, "The list said we could bring a knife for carving."

"Fer *wood*, boy, fer carvin' *wood*. That there thing carves people." He pulled down Ian's collar and added, pointing to the pink scar along his throat, "Seems to me like you oughta know that."

The other boys looked at Ian, who pulled his collar back up, turned his head uncomfortably, and then said, "I didn't see beer on the list." Defiantly determined not to be the only sinner in the crowd, he added, "Or banned books!"

Ackerman swaggered over to Ian and growled lowly, "I tol' you, Eeeon, I don't want no wars. You go upsettin' the natural order a' things in here an' yer a dead man. Now Curt's real good about sharin' his beer and y'all can have a turn with my book when the young'ns is done with it. That way, things stay nice'n copacetic. You got that?"

There it was again . . . the raging glow of his green eyes. It all had to do with the war, Ian thought as he stubbornly nodded in compliance with Ackerman's terms.

For some reason his neck scar ached. Maybe it was the blood pounding through his veins. Maybe it was the fact that the other boys had been staring at it, thinking God knows what. Go ahead, let 'em guess.

Ackerman was smiling malevolently at him now. The grin was so broad he could see the gold fillings in his back teeth. He pulled a cigarette out of his shirt pocket, lit it with a flashy silver-and-turquoise lighter, and exhaled the smoke out the open door. He leaned against the wall and put the hand holding the cigarette out a window.

"Now the rules also says there's no smokin' allowed in the cabins," he explained to Ian. "Rules is rules." He winked to the others. Ian looked at his hand dangling out the window and saw that his fingers were shaking.

Curt placed his hairbrush into his footlocker and said, "I hear they kicked Soleri out."

"That's a fact. Now listen up, men. Here's the bible of the situation. Hyatt ain't gonna let us screw up no more. So playtime's over." He took another drag on his cigarette and looked out over the cove. "Seems ol' Harry's got him this wild hair up his ass to build a fireplace over to the lodge."

"So?" Curt asked.

"So, without no manpower. . . " He said 'maaaaaan-power,' imitating Hyatt's beleaguered speech.

Ian knew where this was going. "You can stop right there, Ackerman. I know what the rest is. You told Hyatt we could build it, didn't you."

Ackerman kept looking out the door and said, "Wasn't no 'could' to it, boy. Tol' him we *would* build it."

"Well, I sure as hell didn't come out here to work on some friggin' chain gang!" Ian grumbled, looking to the others for support.

"Now you jest set an' hear me out, Eeeon."

"Well, it *does* sound like a lot of work, Andy," Curt added cautiously.

"A lot I can do," G'Nat griped, slapping his leg brace.

"Yeah, and I'm too fat for hard labor," Freddy added, happy to have an out.

Ackerman listened patiently, then said, "Y'all done? I knew y'all'd have some questions, so I studied up on it. Now I see it this way: It'll jest be the five a' us, start to finish. Now, since they ain't no buildin' stone around this place, that means we git to go all about lookin' and collectin'. Who knows where that could take us. An' it means we got us our own set a' rules an' hours. Hell, that sounds like money from home to me." He paused, took a drag off his cigarette, blew the smoke out the window, and illustrated the rest of his speech with the arm inside. "I don't know about y'all, but I'm gettin' kinda weary a' all this camp bullshit. I need me a project better'n nature hikes an' leathercrafts." He looked at each boy. "So I tol' Hyatt my hoods could build a fireplace an' chimney better'n anyone else could."

"Oh, so now it's a fireplace *and* a chimney!" Freddy wailed.

"Ain't one much good without t'other."

There was silence as the boys each looked to each other for an opinion. Finally, G'Nat spoke quietly, "I dunno, I kinda like leathercrafts. I still haven't finished that key ring for my foster mom yet."

"Well, we'll take breaks now'n'then. Cain't be all work," Ackerman plied. Silence. "Hell, by my calculations we got us forty-two more days of this! Startin' with that goddam Big Dipper and endin' with, May the Lord bless and keep us, an' I'm gettin' weary of it all!"

"Hold it," Ian broke in. "Do you know one damn thing about building a fireplace?"

"Nope. But Hyatt don't know that. Some high mucky-muck from the board sent out plans. Alls we gotta do is follow 'em. Hell, it's jest rock an' ceement. How hard kin it be?"

"Rock and cement's *real* hard, Andy," Freddy said. "I'm not so sure. . ."

G'Nat poked his finger into Freddy's fleshy arm and asked, "You got any muscle-roony in there?"

Freddy lifted G'Nat's useless leg and let it flop back down with a thud on the bunk. "More'n you got in there."

"Ain't no man expected to do more'n he's able," Ackerman added, his voice gearing down to velvet. "Curt?"

He looked around, then said, "All right, I'm game, since there's no way out anyway. What's McKenzie say?"

All eyes again on him, Ian looked at Ackerman and said, "Look, Ackerman, you better know what the hell you're doing. I'm not breaking my back for this dump."

"That a yes?"

"Yeah, as though I have a real choice."

Ackerman snubbed out his cigarette and said, "Then I reckon we oughta form a partnership." He offered his hand to Freddy, his in turn to G'Nat, his to Curt and then Curt, crossing the room, eye to eye, to Ian. He took it and they shook.

"Thanks for putting my knife away . . . buddy," Ian said, false smile.

"Don't mention it . . . pal," Curt replied, smile just as false.

Then they all looked at Ian and he realized he hadn't completed the circle. He offered his hand to Ackerman, saying, "Shit, why not?"

With the partnership formed, Ackerman popped open Curt's last bottle of beer, held it up, and said, "Here's to chimneys and sech." He took a swig, then passed the bottle around.

eight

Hyatt, Ackerman, and his four charges from Deerslayer stood outside the huge old lodge, slowly looking up at it. The log structure stood two-and-a-half challenging stories.

Ian turned to Curt and asked, "Does the word 'skyscraper' mean anything to you?"

"It sure as hell ain't this big on the inside," Curt said, shading his eyes from the sun as he gazed up.

"Either's our brains for agreeing to this," Freddy grumbled, peeling an orange, gushing a slice, then handing one down to G'Nat.

"I dibs being water boy," G'Nat said.

Hyatt looked equally dubious as he spoke to Ackerman. "I hope I won't regret agreeing to this arrangement . . . How long were you a mason before the war?"

Ackerman looked at Hyatt as though looking for a shred of doubt, and replied, "Hell, if I had me a buck for every foundation I put down, then I'd *buy* y'all a goddam chimney. Thought we'd start this afternoon, providin' you don't mind."

"Just you and these four boys? And one of them a cripple? Why don't you let me recruit some bigger boys from. . . "

"Nope, this here is a Deerslayer project. No more, no less. That's the offer, Harry."

"All right, all right," he said, sounding almost defeated in the face of this sudden good fortune. "Let me get the plans." He walked off, mumbling, "Lord, I hope this works out. . . ."

Curt wandered over to Ackerman and said, "If you were a mason before the war, I was a brain surgeon."

Ackerman's eyes sparkled with sincere gusto at the crack. "Then you got yerself a real fine skill to fall back on, providin' the hoodlum business falls a mite slack."

"How the hell are we going to build a chimney up the side of that thing?" Ian asked, sitting down and looking back up.

"Simple," said Ackerman, "start there," pointing to the ground, "an' end there," pointing to the roof.

"Well, here it is," Hyatt called, handing Ackerman a rolled blueprint of the chimney that had never been built.

Ackerman unrolled it and studied it thoughtfully. "Uh huh. Uh huh. Looks good," he said, turning the blueprint around to view it from several angles. Then he looked up at the lodge as though it all made perfect sense.

"Everything you need is up in the storage shed," said Hyatt. "All the cement, tools, sand, lime, I mean. But like I warned you, you'll have to find and haul the rock. Just outside the cove there's an island that's pretty rocky. You can take one of the boats and haul rock back in it." He paused as he looked up the side of the dining hall, then shook his head sadly and added, "Well, I have to pick up two new board members at the ferry, so I have to rush off." He gave the unlikely looking team a last, apprehensive glance, then added, "Best of luck," before walking off on his rounds.

Ian felt like a B-17 pilot two inches beyond the point of no return.

Ackerman took the blueprint, crumpled it up, and handed it to Freddy, saying, "Here, son, get ridda this. Plans is for sissies. Takes the element a' surprise outa a mission like this. Now, y'all hush an' leave me to study some on this."

Freddy, disgruntled, said, "Thought you already studied on it."

"Shush," Ackerman said, touching Freddy's head as though comforting a toddler.

So while Ackerman studied on it, G'Nat and Freddy pulled out half-finished lanyards and commenced to weave the thin leather strips in, out, under, over. Curt laid back and closed his eyes on the sun, and Ian started throwing rocks into the cove.

After what seemed like an hour, Ackerman announced the end of his studying. Curt, G'Nat, and Freddy sat around him. "Okay now, men, I reckon the best way to go 'bout things is to work in two groups. After lunch, the young'ns'll come with me over to Cracker Bay. Hyatt mentioned they gotta rock man over there an' meybe, if G'Nat an' Freddy here looks real piti-ful, which they got a natural talent for anyhow, I can hustle us a rock donation. Meanwhilst, you older boys take a boat and head for that island Hyatt spoke of."

He looked over toward the water and saw Ian toss-ing rocks into the cove. "You know, Eeeon, I wouldn't

be tossin' them rocks so free-like, being as we're gonna
need alls we can get our hands on, by an' by."

Ian ignored him and kept on throwing. He'd come
close to hitting a buoy parked in the middle of the cove
and he wanted to hit it before he quit.

"Ah, screw him," Curt snapped. "We don't need
him."

But Ian heard him, walked over to where he sat,
dropped a rock dangerously between Curt's legs, and said,
"The hell you don't."

Ackerman watched them, expressionless, as though
he were mentally ringside, calculating the odds between
the champ and his contender.

But Curt just picked up the rock and tossed it into
the woods, where it hit a tree and startled some crows
into flight.

"When you two finally decide to square off, you best
understand there ain't gonna be no stone and there ain't
gonna be no steel. Use yer goddam fists'r I'll kill the
winner. You got that?"

Curt and Ian looked at each other, then back to
Ackerman.

"Good. Jest thought we oughta git that straight,"
Ackerman said, crushing out his cigarette and walking
back down the path.

After lunch, Ian and Curt stood on the dock examining
the inventory of rickety rowboats tied up there. Then
they looked at the lifeless ones overturned on the shore.

"Beats me," Curt said. "They're all lousy. That one

— number nine — on the end, she sinks the slowest. And I think she's a little bigger."

But Ian wasn't listening. He was staring at the Chris Craft moored in the middle of the cove, grinning as he 'studied on it.' Curt followed his gaze.

"You can forget that, McKenzie!" said Curt, joining him at the end of the dock. "That's Hyatt's boat."

"It's for the good of ol' Camp Roswell," Ian said as if arguing his case.

"Look, *I'm* in charge of this operation and I say forget it, or else!"

Ian started loading one of the rowboats with picks, shovels, and gloves, ignoring Curt.

"I mean that's Hyatt's *personal* boat. Touch that, you die. No one's even allowed to swim close to it," Curt tried.

"Chris Craft," Ian said as he admired the boat's shining wood hull. The brass fittings reflected the sun with come-hither flashes.

"Forget it, McKenzie!" Curt warned again.

Ian turned to Curt and growled, "Maybe you Lincoln Lah-lahs ain't as tough as you think. . . "

"Yeah?" Curt replied with equal challenge. "Maybe it's just us Lincoln Lah-lahs're smarter'n you Stadium Softies."

Ian started shedding his sweatshirt, pants, and shoes, and he mumbled, "Go ahead and row. I'm taking the Chris."

"McKenzie. . . ," Curt warned.

But Ian handed his bundle of clothes to Curt and through gritting teeth said, "And you call yourself a

SOK." He turned, dove off the dock, and swam out to the awaiting arms of the Chris.

"You idiot!" Curt called out after him. "You don't even have the key!"

Ian was already into the boat and untying her with the silent speed of a pickpocket. Curt was pacing nervously along the edge of the dock, looking anxiously around for signs of Hyatt, Ackerman, or snitches.

Curt stopped and stared with an amalgam of surprise and wonder as the first, hesitant gurgles escaped the boat's fine inboard engine. Ian eased the Chris around, and as he came alongside the dock he ordered Curt to tie off the rowboat behind as a barge and jump in. Curt hesitated.

"Last chance, Hollenbeck. All it takes is balls."

"Screw you," Curt cursed as he did what he was told. He threw Ian's clothes back down to him, scattering them in the boat. "Just remember, when Hyatt makes us targets on the firing range, this was your idea, not mine."

"Yeah yeah," said Ian, unimpressed. He looked around as he put the boat into gear and added in a thick broguish accent, "Aye, so's the last to die will see the first to go!"

Curt sat down next to Ian, giving the shoreline a last, tentative look. As Camp Roswell grew smaller behind them, the Puget Sound began to appear ahead. Once out of the cove, Ian opened her up and swirled her around to test her agility. The rowboat hung on for the ride of its dear, battered life, and slowly Curt's smile got bigger and more relaxed.

His face spattered with salt water, his sandy hair

windblown, his blue eyes alive with the exuberance of
piracy, Ian looked at Curt and said, shaking his head
pitifully, "And you wanted to row! So where's this rock
island?"

"Ackerman said off to the right. Said we can't miss
it."

"That's starboard, not right, you dope," Ian
corrected.

"I don't care what it is, you're going left."

"That'd be port."

"Wrong way, McKenzie!" Curt called out against the
engine's roar as Ian put more throttle into it. "Come on,
McKenzie, you're going the wrong way."

Ian popped the boat into neutral, and as it coasted
elegantly on its own wake, he stared at his companion
and said, "Look, asshole, this *is* our way!"

"Not for me it isn't! I'm not screwing up my record
for one of your joyrides!"

Ian looked out over the horizon . . . the green holding up the blue, the promise of escape, the city, the
daring. The silvery water beckoned him from every direction but one: the course back to camp.

"Ever been to Bremerton? Naval town. They got
two-for-the-price-of-one whores for every sailor there."

"Turn back, McKenzie. Drop me back at camp, then
you can drive this thing to Timbuktu for all I care!"

Ian looked at Curt incredulously, seeing him in a
different light. He gave him a smile of pity, then shook
his head, put the boat into gear, spun it around, and
headed for the island of rocks. They tied the Chris off

on a dying tree that hung low out over the water, and beached the rowboat.

Since Ian's invitation of piracy and Curt's refusal, they had barely spoken to each other — only under-the-breath curses and insults. But now Ian turned to Curt, took his most impressive street stance, and said, "All right. How about it? No one's around. Wanna have it all out, here and now, Hollenbeck?"

Curt faced the challenge, but didn't respond quick enough for Ian, who came a step closer. He gave him a little push and baited, "No stone, no steel, no witnesses. Come on — you an' me."

Curt shoved back, saying, "Knock it off, jerk!"

But Ian pressed further: "You know, Hollenbeck, you say you're in charge, but I think you're chicken shit."

Curt's face hardened and his eyes grew narrow, but Ian was determined to see how far he could push him. "You know we're going to have it out sooner or later." He backed up, put up his fists, and added, "Let's settle this now. . . "

Curt smiled and said, "Fuck you, Charley. . . " His first punch was hard, full of insulted, budding manhood, and Ian reeled back, shocked at Curt's strength. Maybe this challenge wasn't such a bright idea after all. Before he could recover, Curt got him again, and he tasted warm, salty blood as he staggered back.

Curt was nearly on him for a hat trick when Ian regained his senses and let instinct take over. They parried, swore, spit, swore more, and punched back and forth with equal strength, equal skill. Each warrior had underestimated the other. They fought with abandon, until somebody summoned his uncle from the sky.

Sock. Stumble. Sock. Stumble.

After one too many of these exchanges, exhausted, they fell into the water, barely missing the rowboat. The water, icy, shocking, stunned them both momentarily, and each boy fell back, grasping breath, wiping salt water, sand, and blood from their stinging, battered faces.

They stood up and started again. Their no-witnesses proving ground echoed with groans, grunts, and the unforgiving sound of fist finding face.

Finally, after what seemed like three reels of a John Wayne fight, they each struck out in an exhausted last ditch effort, missed each other clean, and fell into shallow water, half in, half out, numb now to the iciness, the rocks, the heat, the pain.

Eventually, Ian rose on an elbow, looked over to Curt, and said, gasping between each word, "Maybe . . . we . . . shoulda . . . had a . . . witness."

Curt's face, bruised, bloodied, wrinkled into a painful smile. "Maybe next time."

"Okay by me." Ian felt his left eye swelling shut. "Wanna know the pisser?"

"Huh."

"We still gotta fill that goddam boat with rocks. . . "

They looked at the empty boat, which now appeared larger than a barge, and both of them started to laugh.

It took five hours of backbreaking work for the two gladiators to fill the saggy rowboat with stones. They'd started out working separately, silently, each man to his own task, tending his own wounds, his own thoughts. They dug, tugged, jimmied, pulled, strained, swore.

After a few hours, Curt attempted an iceberg of a rock far larger than it appeared above the surface. Ian leaned on his shovel and watched his fellow SOK struggle. Curt attacked the rock with rage, trying to swear it into compliance. Unable to bear that a rock, any rock, even Curt's rock, should not obey, Ian stuck the handle end of his shovel under the rock. Curt pulled and strained until the rock cried uncle, unearthed, and rolled down the embankment toward the rowboat.

The sun beat down on them, but the wind borrowed some of the Sound's coolness and blessed the slow, reluctant, belligerent birth of a team.

Curt looked at the watch he'd borrowed from G'Nat and called over to Ian, "It's almost five-thirty. We better head back."

They sat apart on the beach, surveying their boatload of backbreaking cargo. Ian all but finished the canteen of water, then handed it over to Curt, who thanked him and finished it.

"So, you got your speech ready?" Curt asked, wincing as he splashed Puget Sound water on his blackened, swollen eye.

Ian threw his gloves into the Chris, soaked his hands in the cool salt water, and asked, "What speech?"

"To Hyatt. What are you going to tell him?"

"Screw Hyatt."

"Your funeral."

"Yep."

They sank into the comfort of the sun-warmed

leather seats, each boy aching to the bone, trying to appear as fit and strong as when they first started. Ian carefully eased the Chris out, watching their loaded rowboat follow.

They motored leisurely into the cove where Ackerman, Freddy, and G'Nat were sitting on the beach awaiting their return. The rest of the camp was up at the lighting ritual before dinner.

Crawling along with their resisting cargo in tow, they eased the rowboat in close to the shore. Silently, Ackerman waded out and pulled it in, glaring when his eyes met Ian's and Curt's. With a grateful moan, the rowboat beached.

After securing the Chris to her mooring buoy, both Ian and Curt dived into the water for a refreshing, stinging swim back to shore. Once on shore, they looked down with pride on their boatload of rocks.

Freddy stared at the two red, swollen, dripping boys. "Jesus H. Christ, what happened to you two?"

"The rocks didn't want to come," Ian replied casually as he gently dried his face.

Curt asked Freddy, "How'd you guys do?"

G'Nat looked at each elder, then said, "Helluva lot better'n you two. You look like raw hamburger."

"Some guy gave *us* a whole truckload," said Freddy. He pointed quickly to Ackerman, who had by now walked out to the end of the dock and was staring out at Hyatt's commandeered Chris Craft. He took an odd, at-ease stance, cigarette dangling off his lip.

Curt and Ian looked at each other, then out at Ackerman. "What's with Laughing Boy?" Ian asked.

"Hyatt came down with two bigwigs from the board to take them for a ride in his boat this afternoon," Freddy explained. His perpetually sunburned face was solemn, as though he'd just announced another attack on Pearl Harbor.

"Goddam it, McKenzie!" Curt said. "Let's see you fight your way out of this."

"Been nice knowing you," G'Nat said, limping over to the older boys. He turned to Freddy, put his hand on his shoulder, and added, "Guess it's just you and me now, ol' pal, ol' budd-a-roony. Can I have your ration coupons, Curt?"

"He chewed Ackerman a new asshole," Freddy continued, ignoring G'Nat's sarcasm.

"What did Ackerman tell him?" Curt asked.

"I don't know. G'Nat and me, we exodust like slick."

"Been nice knowing you," G'Nat repeated.

Ian began walking toward Ackerman. But when Curt followed, Ian turned and said, "Stay out of it, Hollenbeck. I took the boat, I'll take the heat. I don't want to screw up your precious record."

Ian walked boldly to the end of the dock. He stood next to Ackerman, but didn't look at him. "So, Hyatt's pissed, eh?"

"Stow it! I got ya off the hook, boy," Ackerman returned coldly, taking a drag off his cigarette and keeping his eyes on the Chris.

"Well, no one asked you to. I took Hyatt's goddam boat and I'll own up to it. I can take the heat!"

"I took the gunfire, boy," Ackerman said, almost to himself.

Ian, angered, pulled Ackerman around to face *him*, not the damn Chris Craft, and shouted, "Hyatt said to take one of the boats! The key was right there in it! Using that boat was the fastest way I could think of to haul his goddam rock for his goddam fireplace!"

Ackerman flicked his cigarette into the water and replied, "Convenient, ain't it?"

Now Ian was pointing a finger at Ackerman. The other three SOKs stood silent on the shore. "Look, mister, I said I can take the heat for anything I do!"

Ackerman looked at the pointing finger as though he'd just as soon rip it out of its socket as have it continue to point so impudently. Ian put his hand down and added, "So, I'll just hand Hyatt my resignation and you know what you can do with all that fucking rock!"

"Easy, boy," Ackerman whispered, looking down and dusting Ian's shoulder. "There's that ol' chip again. Makin' you six feet above contradictions. Ya said yer piece, an' now it's over. Let's go eat. We got us a lotta rock to tote." He started back up the dock.

"So what about Hyatt?" Ian asked, an expression of cooled anger on his sunburned face.

"He's pliable as a wad a' wax on a summer's day," Ackerman replied. Ian followed behind in order to hear him. "I convinced him you men showed lotsa 'nitiative, an' if his boat kin help the project along, then more power to us. Only tell him when yer takin' it, boy. That's all."

He stopped, smiled wickedly down at Ian, and added, "Shore was a sight seein' ol' Hyatt row them two hotshots 'round the cove in one a' them derelicts. Oh, an' one more thing: I ever see y'all taking that Chris fer yer own pleasure, y'all might jest as well keep on headin' out to sea."

Curt had come up from the beach and was standing next to Ian. Ackerman looked at each boy, then walked around them as though taking inventory of their battle scars.

"Who won?" he asked clinically.

Both Ian and Curt pointed to the other.

"Anybody need stitchin'?"

For the first time, Ian and Curt looked closely at each other's handiwork and replied together, "Nah."

Ackerman just turned and walked away, shaking his head, and the two other SOKs scrambled close to the dock.

"You kicked out?" Freddy asked.

Ian kept watching Ackerman as he disappeared into the forest. "He's one tough son of a bitch to figure out."

"I could have told you that," Curt said. Then, to the two lesser SOKs, "Bring those tools up here, you twerps."

"Bring 'em yourself, asshole!" G'Nat snapped back, with Freddy as his shield. Curt's glare countered.

"All right, all right," Freddy said, hauling G'Nat back down to the beach and the equipment.

Without a doubt, it had been the longest day of his life. Ian lay awake on his bunk listening to the rhythmic breathing of the other Deerslayer boys. His body ached so much, he doubted he would ever fall asleep. He relived his day from the predawn ferry ride to the Big Dipper initiation, the expulsion of Soleri, the fight for superiority, and the shelling he had taken on the dock. You've had a hard day, cowboy . . . the last words his father had said to him seven, no, it was eight years ago. Half my life ago, Ian thought. Dad's been gone half my life. You've had a hard day, cowboy. . .

He fell asleep trying to remember the color of his father's eyes, and unable to forget the glaring, daring green of Ackerman's.

nine

The boys agreed to name the rocky island Alcatraz, for during the following week Curt and Ian were sentenced every day to hard labor on that scrubby little piece of land.

Ian taught G'Nat how to drive the Chris. G'Nat's job was operating the barge service between the island and camp, while Freddy and Ackerman unloaded rocks from the rowboats and hauled them in rickety old wheelbarrows from the beach up to the lodge, where they formed a mountain of precious stone.

After a boat was unloaded, and before he had to go pick up another load, G'Nat scoured the many streams around camp for small, smooth river rocks to form the mantel ledge and grace the mighty hearth. Ackerman had fashioned G'Nat a canvas sack, which he strung around his neck. Despite his leg brace, he searched tirelessly.

They were indeed free from the regimen of camp life, but after the first blistering day, if any one of them thought the job would be a breeze, they knew they had been sadly, and sorely, mistaken. In the evenings, they cooled off in the waters of the cove, devoured double rations, surveyed the day's accomplishments, and set goals for the next day.

Day by day, the boys of Deerslayer, the SOKs —

the 'special needs' boys — became increasingly the unhailed heroes of the camp. When it became apparent that a man-sized task was unfolding, the SOKs were given a wider berth by most of the camp regulars. If another camper came across a rock in his daily routine, he would dig it up and add it to the mountain.

At the end of the first week, while the rest of the campers were offering their nightly songs to the gods of the campfire, Ackerman led his crew down to the rock mountain. They made a crude measure of the pile to determine its cubic worth.

"Where's the blueprint, Freddy?" Ackerman finally asked, between his lips a stubby pencil rather than the habitual cigarette.

"You told me to throw it away!" Freddy said in a high-pitched voice of self-defense.

Ackerman took the pencil out of mouth and said, "Since when you ever done what I tol' you?"

"Sor-ry," Freddy grumbled unapologetically.

"Never mind. Jest wanted to see if their calculations was right, anyhow."

He made some more sketches on his clipboard, calculating out loud while the boys sat down in the cool, damp grass.

He finally announced, after lighting a cigarette, "I reckon we got jest 'bout half a' what we'll be needin'." He took his measuring tape and chalked off a ten foot base on the side of the lodge.

His announcement was accompanied by a cacophony of moans.

Ian fell back and covered his eyes with his blistered

hands. "Half? Oh God, I'm not going to live to see this thing finished!"

"You?" Freddy demanded in the spirit of one-upsmanship. "I'll bet I've lost fifty pounds! My mom won't recognize me at this rate!"

"Lucky for her!" G'Nat chipped in.

"Cora Lee won't let these hands touch her again!" Curt added, looking at his rough, red hands.

"Coooraaaaa Leeeeee?" Freddy and G'Nat teased in unison.

"Yeah, Cora Lee!" Curt said. "Look, I didn't name her, so lay off."

"Curt's got squirrel fever for Coooora Leeeee!" G'Nat teased further.

Ian silenced them, pointing to Ackerman, who was walking around the rock pile talking and calculating to himself, pausing occasionally to take a thoughtful drag on his cigarette and disagree or agree with himself. Finally he looked over to Ian and asked, "How's Alcatraz lookin' fer rock?"

"We take one more rock off of Alcatraz, she'll float away," Ian muttered, his hands back over his eyes.

"Oh, sure!" G'Nat said, shoving Ian.

"Jesus Christ, Ackerman, Ian's right," Curt said, leaning back on his elbows. "We got all the loose rock we could find. Next step would be excavation, and I got news for you, the only thing I have the strength to dig now is my own grave."

Ian lifted his hands enough to look at Curt and quipped, "Make it a double."

"Well, what about that guy over in Cracker Bay?

Maybe he'll give us some more rocks, being as it's such a good cause and all," Freddy offered hopefully.

"He was hard pressed to spare us that," Ackerman said. "Cain't go askin' twice."

"Then why can't Hyatt and some of his high-falooting buddies from Tacoma chip in and buy the rest?" Ian asked, now looking up into the gently swaying shadows of the pine trees.

"Nope. Nope," Ackerman said with resolve. "We'll jest keep lookin', that's all. Tomorrow, G'Nat, Freddy, an' me, we'll start cuttin' away fer the firebox. Curt, you an' Eeeon. . . "

"We know, we know. . . " Curt began, followed by Ian. "Al-ca-traaaa. . . "

Late that night, long after Taps, long after the campfire had bowed out, long after the moon had risen high above the lazy cove, Ian lay awake on his upper bunk. He stared for some time at the dancing sprites of reflected water on the ceiling, trying to pick up a rhythm, a pattern, a symmetry to the dance. He leaned his head back and looked, upside down, at Curt's head on his bunk.

"Hollenbeck?" he whispered to the still head.

"What?" Curt whispered back, not moving.

"You awake?"

"What'd you think?"

"You tired of Alcatraz?"

"I'd just as soon check into the *real* one. . . "

"Yeah. Me too," Ian whispered.

The cabin was silent, except for the sound of gently lapping waves. Curt whispered, "Face it, we're stuck."

"*You* might be. . . " Ian whispered back. Even in a whisper, Curt recognized the taunt, the dare, in Ian's voice. He rolled over and looked at Ian with suspicion.

"What the hell you thinking, McKenzie?"

Ian raised himself up on his elbows and looked down at Freddy and G'Nat's bunks below. "Hey, Freddy, you awake?"

The reply came in the form of a kick from below and Freddy's grumbling voice, "No, so why don't you two guys shut up. I need my beauty sleep."

Ian leaned over his bunk and threatened, "Kick me again and I'll make sure you never eat another marshmallow as long as you live."

"Without marshmallows he won't live very long," Curt intercepted.

Ian looked over to Curt, smiled wickedly, and said, "Well then, it solves both problems."

"Screw you!" Freddy said. "It's almost eleven. Ackerman gets back here and finds you awake, he'll crap."

The three settled back down. Soon, Ian could tell by the deep, even breaths of Freddy below that he had fallen asleep. Then Ian heard the sound of soft footsteps on the porch, followed by the squeak of the rocker and the unmistakable snap of Ackerman's silver lighter.

A somehow soothing sound, the gentle back and forth of the rocker, the porch sweetly acquiescing underneath. Then Ackerman began to hum. Shyly at first, an almost familiar strain. . .

Ian opened his eyes to listen closer.

". . . and then she takes my hand . . . da, da, da, daaaaaa, da, da, da, daaaaaa . . . and then I understand . . . da, da, daaaaaa, da, da, da, daaaaaa. . . "

Ian turned toward the window and looked down on Ackerman as he sat, sang, smoked. He thought about telling him to knock it off already, then thought better of it and lay back down to listen.

Then, seductively, as the melody grew ever so slightly. . .

". . . she takes me to Paaaaar-AAAAAA-diiiiiise. . . "

Then three more rocks, then footsteps back down the steps.

Ian reached over his head, tapped Curt's pillow, and whispered, ever so lowly, "You awake, Curt?"

"Yeah. . . "

"His voice ain't half bad. . . "

"Yeah. I just wish he knew another song."

Ian looked out the window to make sure Ackerman was gone and asked, "You think Ackerman is taking this thing . . . this chimney thing a little too seriously?"

Curt opened his eyes, paused, and asked, "What do you mean?"

"I keep finding him staring at the lodge and then at the rocks. Shit, Curt, a rock's a rock. I saw him staring at one rock yesterday, just turning it over and over like he was looking for something on it. Hell, he might even have been carrying on a conversation with it for all I know. I got a feeling all the rocks we need are in his head. The guy's wacko."

Again Curt paused before replying, "Maybe he just

needs this project to, you know, get his mind off other things. Like maybe the war?"

Ian looked again at the moon-sent beams swaying on the ceiling and felt himself being seduced toward sleep. He cradled his head on his arms, closed his eyes, and replied, "Yeah. Maybe." Then, with eyes still closed, he asked, "Hey, Hollenbeck, you got an alarm on your clock?"

"Yeah, why?"

"Set it for four, will you?"

Curt whirled over and pulled Ian's pillow out from under his head. "Why? What for? What're you up to, McKenzie?"

Ian reached out, grabbed his pillow back, and said quite plainly, "I'm taking the camp truck."

"Where to? No, don't tell me, I don't want to know! You're on your own, I mean *really* on your own this time, McKenzie!"

"Relax, hotshot, I'm not taking a hike. I'm going to find Ackerman the rest of his friggin' rocks."

"Hyatt'll kick us all out, McKenzie, you know he wi. . . "

"Hyatt's gone. This is Friday. Where does he spend every Friday night? With his mommy in Gorst, right, Bright Boy? I'll be back before he unloads his ol' lady's groceries."

"Yeah, well what about Ackerman?"

"What the hell are you worried about? A: he sleeps like lead, and B: he hardly sleeps here anyway."

"No, I mean if you get caught? It's *his* ass on the line too, you know."

"So I'll leave him a note pinned to his 'jammies. That way, if I get caught," he looked at Curt upside down, "which I won't, he'll have proof it was all my doing."

Curt flopped back down into his bunk and then was silent for a while. Then, "You know how to hot wire?"

Ian smiled to the ceiling. "All it takes is one little ol' gum wrapper."

"Stealing a truck is grand theft, you know. . . "

"Oh, it'll be grand, all right," Ian said confidently. "So, you with me?"

"You sure you know how to drive?"

Ian's grin grew bigger and he closed his eyes as though looking back on many a joy ride. "Like Barry Oldfield," he whispered, the voice of the tempter.

"Aw shit," Curt said with a resigned hiss. He reset his alarm clock, stuffed it under his pillow, then punched the pillow a few times for comfort, flopped over on his side, and reiterated, barely audible, "Aw shit. . . "

ten

Curt and Ian both pounced on the alarm clock the moment it signaled four o'clock. Startled awake, they looked at each other wide-eyed and, for an instant, wondered who they were, where they were, and why any of it mattered?

Ian looked down at Ackerman's empty bunk and gave Curt an I-told-you-so grin.

They were up and out of the cabin in a matter of silent seconds, and sneaking down toward the maintenance shed. Using a flashlight, also stolen, they crept into the shed. There parked, patiently awaiting the call to the next camp duty, was the truck, ancient, dented, loyal, and duly identified as CAMP ROSWELL on its doors. Curt shined the light inside the cab.

Curt handed the flashlight to Ian, patted his shirt pockets, and whispered, "Shit, I think I lost the gum. . . "

But Ian was way ahead of him. "Never mind, these idiots leave the keys in the ignition. God, they're a bunch of saps out here!"

"Yeah, lucky for you."

Ian jumped in the cab and released the hand brake. Curt jumped in next to him. Ian looked at him like he too was an idiot. "What do you think *you're* doing?"

"I'm helping you steal a goddam truck, what'd you think. . . "

"Get out and push this thing! I start it up here, the whole camp'll wake up. Once you get it rolling, run ahead and open the gate. I'll start 'er up when we're outside," Ian explained as though he was talking to a first grader. "See how that works?"

Curt shoved the door open and grumbled, "Yeah, *now* I know why you wanted me along!"

"Curt?" Ian called out the window.

Curt came back and snapped, "What?"

"Don't you think you'll want to see where you're going?"

Curt grabbed the flashlight and went back to the hood of the truck. Ian looked at Curt, who grunted and growled, his shoulder hard against the hood of the truck. It didn't budge. Ian tried not to laugh at Curt's eyes bulging, cheeks puffed out. "Look, could I get some help here, asshole?" he finally demanded.

Ian joined him, and together they pushed the truck out of its sandy berth in the shed. Once it was moving, Ian leaped into the driver's seat, but controlling the truck as it rolled downhill — backwards — in the dark — was a feat even Barry Oldfield would have liked to see. The hill was steeper than anticipated, and Curt had to sprint to avoid being run over by the truck as it sped toward the gate, the flashlight bobbing its weak light as he ran. Curt scrambled, swearing, as he found the latch and opened the gate just as the truck careened through. Once on the road, Ian had to pump the brakes to stop. Then he started the hesitant engine. He turned on the headlights, which were weak as the brakes and offered only slight assistance.

"Thought you could run faster'n that," Ian griped as Curt jumped in. "You'd make a stupid hood ornament. Get it? You? J.D.? *Hood* ornament?"

Curt stared coldly at Ian as he caught his breath, saying, "Yeah yeah, I get it. You damn near ran me over! See that pedal right there? It's called a brake and it works whether or not the friggin' engine's running, jerk!"

"Well, not necessarily on this piece of shit, but let's not worry about details," Ian said. He looked into the darkness around them and asked, "Well, which way? All I know is Mexico's that way and Canada's that way."

"How much bug juice in this thing?" Curt asked, casing the dashboard with the flashlight.

"Christ! This thing's almost empty!" Ian said, slapping the steering wheel. "Shoulda figured any idiot who leaves keys in the ignition doesn't keep the damn tank topped."

"No gas? You're kidding!"

"Well, unless 'E' stands for E-nough, this could be a short trip," Ian barked back.

"Look, take a right. We'll head to Cracker Bay and get some gas, that's all," Curt explained.

"With what, our good looks?"

Curt rummaged through his pockets and pulled out some change, "I have a little money for the camp store. No green stuff, but. . . "

"So big deal. Got any gas ration coupons?"

"Oh, I forgot," Curt said, a frown of angry disappointment on his face.

"How could you forget there's a war?" Ian demanded.

"Because that's what I'm out here for!" Curt snapped defensively.

Ian looked over at him. Curt had his arms folded protectively in front of him. He knew immediately what Curt was talking about.

"You? A badgy? No way you could pass for eighteen, Hollenbeck."

"They're takin' 'em at seventeen now."

"You barely look sixteen."

"Cora Lee thinks. . . " then he caught himself.

"Hold it, I know the rest: Cora Lee thinks you'd look cute as a cap pistol in a uniform, right?" Ian kept his eyes on the dirt road ahead.

"Just shut up about it, okay?" Curt bristled. He sank down deeper into the seat.

"I can see the headlines now: Tacoma Kid Kills Krauts. True Age Revealed. Gets Screwed."

"I said, shut up!"

But Ian couldn't let go. A charming grin of discovery spread across his face and he wanted Curt to confess more. "How many times did you try?"

"I said, drop it!"

"Listen, on my side of town a boy ain't a man unless he tries to enlist. . . "

"You know, you're just like my mother. Jaws of a bulldog! Once you get a hold of something, you can't let go!"

They continued in silence. Bouncing with the chucks in the road, Ian had to hang onto the wheel to keep his balance. He decided to let Curt's dander keep bouncing about the cab of the truck for a while.

Then, unable to keep a smirk off his face, Ian turned to Curt and confessed, "I tried the Navy, the Army . . . and the USO"

"The *USO?*" Curt bellowed, finally looking at him. "What the hell were you going to do for them, sell dance tickets?"

"Well," Ian explained sheepishly, ". . . that was right after Pearl Harbor. I was just a kid. Some jerk told me that USO. stood for United States Officers. You know, sort of a direct line into the upper ranks. . . "

"I can't believe you were that stupid!" Curt bellowed, slipping down into his seat in hysteria.

"Hey, give me a break, I was just a stupid kid. Anyway, I go waltzing into the USO thinking I'd walk out a general or something. . . " Curt's laughter was so contagious, Ian found himself laughing as he recounted the episode.

"And. . . ?" Curt demanded, his dark eyes alive with aroused curiosity.

"Well," Ian said, trying to hold back his laughter, "when that old bat at the check-in table started laughing at me, I came unhinged. I have this little anger problem, you know." Then, in Ackerman's Southern drawl, he continued, "Yup son, what follered warn't a purdy sight. . . "

"What follered?"

"I did have my pride, you know. . . ," he baited.

"What the hell happened?" he demanded.

"I told her I didn't care if she *was* Father Flanigan's

mistress, she was a goddam lying whore and I knew why she worked at the USO!"

Curt was doubled over with laughter. "You're a lying son of a bitch!"

"It's true, I swear, every word of it!" He crossed his heart.

"So what finally happened?"

"She slapped me. I kicked her. She screamed. I swore. Some gorilla grabbed me by the collar and lifted me clean off the ground, giving me a nice direct line to his nuts. Got him square. Needless to say, he immediately dropped me and I cut out like hell. From that day on, I knew the USO wasn't the branch for me."

They rode on in silence. Slowly, the smiles faded.

"Think you'll ever join the service?" Curt asked, looking out the window for more road signs.

"I live for the day I can get out of Tacoma."

"Yeah, me too."

"You wanna know what's really stupid?"

"Stupider than the USO thing?" Curt asked, realizing he hadn't ever heard quite that tone in Ian's voice before.

"Yeah, stupider."

"What?"

"For a time I wanted to go to Annapolis — be a Naval Cadet. Thought that'd be really prime. More'n anything else in the world. How's that for stupider?"

Curt laughed and looked out the window, confessing, "I wanted West Point. I think it was the uniform."

"I even went to the counselor's office at school."

"No shit? On purpose?"

"Yeah. Bastard laughed."

"It's their job with the likes of us," Curt said, looking at his reflection in the window, running his fingers through his rumpled hair. "So what'd he tell you?"

"Said the only way I could get to Annapolis, even if I kept my grades four-0 and my nose clean. . . "

He looked at Ian and asked, "*Kept* four-0? You mean straight A's? You smart or something?"

Ian hadn't intended on letting it out, so he casually replied, "Nah, just lucky. Anyway, this counselor said I'd have to be *nominated* to Annapolis by a governor or senator or God."

"It's their way of keeping guys like us out. I kissed off West Point."

Suddenly, the company couldn't be better. Ian further confessed, "Yeah. Oh, he told me sometimes some hotshot military guy like a Medal of Honor winner or something could pull a few strings. Now, I ask you, what do you do? Go down to the Big Fuckin' Heroes Union Hall and hire some ol' doughboy to write a letter?"

They laughed and Curt added, "Yeah, the B.F.H.! Look, McKenzie, like I told you, they don't want our likes. So screw 'em."

"Yeah, screw 'em."

They rode in silence until, out of nowhere, Ian remarked casually, "I think my dad's in the Navy."

"You *think*? You don't *know*?"

"Who knows. He took a hike when I was a kid."

"Too bad."

"Hey, there's an advantage to that. I can make him anything I want him to be."

"Freddy'd have him Commander in Chief or a Sheik of Ar-a-beek," Curt said.

"So, what's your old man do?"

"He was a janitor. But now he's in the Army. Italy I think. He doesn't write much."

"Yeah, I think my ol' man's a captain or a commander or something," Ian said, nodding his head wisely.

More distance. More silence. More bravado building.

Curt continued, "Yeah. I quit thinking West Point last year. Now, I just want a straight shot into the action. Screw that officer shit. Just give me a gun and let me fight!" He held an imaginary machine gun and blooeed a line of Japs.

"Yeah, I told Senator Magnuson he'd have to find some other lackey to nominate to Annapolis," Ian added.

"Screw 'em all, right?"

"Right. But I'll tell you this: I don't care if I'm only a mop-jockey, I'm sailing out of Tacoma faster'n you can say MacArthur."

"That'll be me passing you," Curt added.

"No way. I've seen you run, Hollenbeck. G'Nat could pass me before you could!"

Ian pulled the truck onto an off-road, and the boys caught some sleep so that when the sun had risen, bearings could be found, gas could be procured, and adventure could be had.

eleven

Ian sprang awake with the first ray of light on the dash-board. He pulled Curt awake, and they resumed their journey.

The small fishing village of Cracker Bay appeared before them, sprawling casually, shining sweetly in the morning sun. Ian pulled the truck to a stop, then backed into a driveway well hidden by trees.

"What're you doing?" Curt asked, looking around.

"Getting gas."

"But the station's up there, if anywhere," Curt pointed to the town ahead. "Besides, we don't have any coupons."

"Don't need 'em. I got an idea. There's a gas can in the back. . . "

Curt's face lit up and he asked, "A gas can in the back? Why the hell didn't you say so earlier?" He leaped out of the truck, opened the gas can, then frowned up at Ian. "Empty."

"What, you think I didn't already check that?" Ian asked, looking at Curt with a parental scowl. "Now grab that thing and follow me. Look tired," Ian instructed as he jumped out of the truck.

Ian was explaining his plan when they reached the

gas station. "Hell, they're not even open," Curt protested. "This is stupid."

"Even better," Ian said. He kicked some dust onto Curt's shoes and pants. "Here, do me. We have to look road-weary. Better yet, ditch your shoes." Ian slipped off his sneakers and tossed them into the brush.

"Whatever it is, it'll never work," Curt said, following suit.

"Trust me."

For an hour, they loitered in front of the gas station, dusty, barefoot, waiting for the attendant to open up. Ian sat on the large red gas can, and Curt nervously paced around the pumps.

Finally, an old man came, unlocked the doors, and went about switching on the two pumps and looking the boys over carefully.

"Morning, sir," Ian said, standing up. "Excuse me, do you have the time?"

He pulled out a watch from his pants pocket and said, "Seven oh two."

Ian turned to Curt and said, "See, Burt, I told you we could make it in two hours."

"You boys need some gas?" the man asked, looking at the gas can.

"Boy, we sure do. We're from Camp Roswell. The camp truck ran out of gas back at camp and we volunteered to walk to town and pick some up," Ian explained smoothly.

"Camp Roswell, eh? That's quite a piece down the road, son. You boys walked?" He started to fill the can.

"Yes, sir. Made it in less than two hours. Anyway,

Mr. Hyatt — he's the camp man — said to go ahead and charge it to the camp," Ian continued.

The man clicked off the pump and stood up, holding the hose upright. "I'm sorry, son, Camp Roswell doesn't have an account here."

Ian looked at Curt, then innocently back at the man. "But Mr. Hyatt, he said the gas station at Shady Creek carried the account. He told Burt an' me to. . . "

"Shady Creek?" the man repeated. "I'm sorry, boys, but this is Cracker Bay. You've walked the wrong way!"

Ian and Curt again exchanged downhearted, exhausted glances. "Oh no," Curt said helplessly, slapping his hand to his forehead.

Ian looked at the gas can and said with a sad sigh, "Guess you better pour what's in there out. Well, Burt, looks like. . . "

"Oh now, hold on, boys. . . " the man said, a look of genuine concern in his eyes. "Look, I'll fill your can. Tell your camp director to come on in and settle up. I hate to think of you boys coming all this way. . . "

Ian's face brightened. "Say, mister, that's real swell. Thanks."

"In fact, I'll go you one better. That can will be too heavy for you two to carry all that way. . . "

"Oh, we wouldn't hear of it!" Ian broke in, reading his mind.

"But, son, that's a twenty-gallon can you have there. It'd take six of you to walk all the way back to Camp Roswell with that," the man protested.

"Nah, we can do it," Ian said. "This is our job. We volunteered for it."

"Yeah, it's like a mission. A camp mission," Curt

added, screwing the lid on the gas can and trying to pick it up.

Ian helped him lift it and said, grinning, "You know, you've done more than enough already, mister. See? Light as a feather." He tried to transform the strain on his face to a smile. He looked at Curt, whose face registered equal strain, and said, "Gee, Burt, now we'll get our hiking badges!"

"It won't take long to run you on out there," the man insisted, patting his pockets in search of his keys.

"No, no," Curt said, a somber look on his face. When he wanted to, Ian noticed, Curt could look downright catastrophic. "This is a Camp Roswell pledge: never start something you can't finish."

"But. . . " The man watched helplessly as the two boys backed away with the large, cumbersome can.

"Boys Into Men. Camp motto. Thank you. Mr. Hyatt will settle up later," Ian said, waving good-bye to the attendant.

Once around the corner, the boys set the container down and exhaled their exhaustion.

"Christ on a crutch, that's heavy!" Ian said, looking at the dent the wire handle had made in his palm.

"You're smooth, McKenzie. Real smooth. I don't know why the USO didn't want you."

"Ah, I'm a lousy dancer."

They retrieved their sneakers, filled the tank, and then Ian started up the truck. Watching the gauge slowly climb to 'F', he pointed to it and said brightly, "There now, 'F' for Fun. Let's go!"

As they drove past the gas station attendant in town, they waved cheerfully. The man absently waved back, and it wasn't until they were well past him that Ian saw him, in the rearview mirror, throw his hat down in the anger of being had.

It was one of the finer joy rides Ian had ever taken. The '34 Ford truck did its gallant best, squirreling around the old country roads with the heart of a roadster, leaving a screen of smoky dust in its wake. One-eighties, three-sixties, burning the breeze down endless, dusty, hair-pinned roads. But by ten, the gas gauge was working its way past the halfway mark and the boys decided it best to get their day's mission underway.

"Do you have any idea where we are?" Curt finally asked, looking around for a familiar speck of land. "We've been in these woods a while, you know."

"Wasn't there a Puget Sound somewhere in these parts?" Ian asked, beginning to take their dense green surroundings a little more seriously.

Ian swirled the truck in a wide, sudden circle, hanging onto the large steering wheel as they spun about.

"Okay, Barry Oldfield!" Curt protested as he slammed up against the door. "Give a guy some warning, will you?" He fanned away some dust, which fluffed into the cab.

"Sorry," Ian said, flooring the pedal and leaning intensely into the wheel.

"Take that road!" Curt shouted, pointing past Ian's face. They came to a slamming halt, backed up, then swung around and took Curt's road.

Curt pointed to a lopsided road sign that offered their alternatives: Shady Creek, six miles that way,

Cracker Bay, sixteen miles that way and Excelsior three miles straight ahead.

"Excelsior? That I gotta see," Ian said. "We can't go back without seeing the sights of Excelsior!"

The tall fir trees that guarded each side of the road gradually began to grow thinner until they surrendered entirely to gently rolling pastures. Ian stopped the truck at the foot of a long driveway that ostentatiously led to a palace of a farmhouse atop a distant hill.

"You looking at what I'm looking at?" Ian asked Curt.

"Yeah. Nice joint," Curt replied, looking at the white, pristine homestead.

"Not the house, you dope! Right there! Look at the wall." Ian pulled Curt by the shirt and forced him to look just beyond the nose of the truck.

It was magnificent. Four feet high, two wide, and lining the entire distance of the driveway, the rockery served as both fence and warning.

"Well, where there's rock, there's rock," Ian said wisely.

"I'm afraid to ask why we're going up here," Curt said, slumping back with a sigh of resignation while Ian drove up the driveway.

It only took Ian a few minutes to negotiate with the woman of the house. Yes, they did have all the rock Camp Roswell could possibly need for their fireplace and probably six more, and no, it wouldn't cost a thing.

"Okay, let me have it. How'd you wrangle this one?" Curt demanded as Ian began to back the truck around to a huge rock pile by a geese-ladened pond.

"See all those trees up there?" He pointed to a hillside of Christmas trees. "Well, in case you forgot again, there's a war on and the ol' lady doesn't have anyone to prune her trees. . . "

"No way, McKenzie. I'm no lumberjack!"

"You know, you're going to get an ulcer, you worry so much. I told the ol' lady Camp Roswell would send out ten strong boys to prune her goddam Christmas trees, so what d'you think about that?" Ian said matter-of-factly. He pulled up the hand brake, grabbed his gloves, and added, "Are you going to get out and help, or do you wanna prune Christmas trees?"

With the truck loaded to the gills with rock — cream-colored rocks of good, sturdy size and shape — Ian had to drive the truck with a measure of sanity. As they entered the town of Shady Creek, Ian remembered staples were low in their footlockers.

He pulled the truck up in front of a small country store and looked at Curt.

"Now what?" Curt asked, his face full of suspicion.

"Just need to pick up a few things."

"McKenzieeeeee. . . "

But Ian was out of the truck before Curt could register further misgivings.

He returned a few moments later, seemingly empty-handed.

"I knew you couldn't pull this one off," Curt said.

Then Ian turned and said, quite earnestly, "Don't you think it's better to try and fail than never to try at all?" His face, streaked with dried sweat and dirt, was solemnly gray, accentuating his light blue eyes. Then his face lit up and he opened his coat, displaying four large quart bottles of beer tucked into his pants.

"Christ, these're cold!" He pulled himself into the truck, popped one with a church key he kept in his pants pocket, gulped some, and offered it to Curt. "Beer, son?" Then from his jacket pocket he took out a box and handed it to Curt. "Look, I even found some marshmallows for Freddy. . . " Another pocket. ". . . a candy bar for G'Nat. . . " He started the truck and extracted from his shirt pockets two packs of Camel cigarettes. Curt watched in amazement. ". . . and two herds for Ackerman."

"You swiped all this?" Curt asked, looking at the loot stacked in his lap.

Ian paused to enjoy Curt's expression and said, "Well, not exactly. I charged it."

"To who?"

"Harry Hyatt, who else?"

"They let you charge beer and smokes?"

"Well," Ian admitted, taking another swig of beer. "Those were an afterthought. . . "

They passed the beer and rode in silence as each boy began to let the events of the day fall into proper order and perspective. They were exhausted, yet exuberant, each in his own way, from the day's adventures.

Finally, not far from the winding road into Camp Roswell, Curt asked, "How do you do it, McKenzie?"

"Do what?"

"Always get away with everything."

"Hell. . . " Ian replied, feeling his back straighten as Curt approached this delicate area. "I get caught just like everybody else. You're just seeing me on a lucky day. All this will catch up with me. God, will it catch up with me." He would rather die than let Curt know that all he was doing, or ever wanted to do, was outdo, outshine, and impress everyone . . . in this case, Curt, the boys of Deerslayer and, goddam it, even that wacko Ackerman.

Suddenly Ian slammed on the brakes to avoid hitting a dog that had run out of the woods and dashed in front of the truck. The tail end of the truck swerved, but Ian brought the loaded vehicle under control, pulled the hand brake, watched the dust settle around them, and said in a shaky whisper, "Je-sus Chr-ist!"

"Did we miss him?" Curt asked, leaping out of the truck.

When they found him, the dog was lying on the side of the road, panting so hard his mouth appeared to be grinning at the shaken boys as though to say, "That was fun. Let's do it again!"

"Here, boy. . . " Curt called, holding his hand out to entice the dog. "I don't think we hit him. Come here, boy. . . "

"Ugly son of a bitch," Ian said, looking at the dog's odd coat of gray and black spots. "I've seen slugs with better markings."

When the dog rose to accept Curt's offer of friendship, both boys were surprised to see the dog had only three legs.

"Look at that!" Curt said. "Three legs! What do you know?"

"He must have been going for two, the way he came at us like that," Ian said. "Come on. He's okay. . . . Let's go. You wanna swim, remember?" He started to climb back aboard the truck.

"He must be lost," Curt insisted, petting the dog fondly. The dog, still panting, sidled into Curt's legs, enjoying the affection.

"Aw, he's someone's farm dog. Come on, Hollenbeck, get in the truck. I'm leaving," Ian called, standing on the running board.

"I'll bet no one lives around here for miles. I'm taking him back to camp." He slapped his leg and the dog willingly followed, his one front leg working perfectly in rhythm with his hind two.

Curt lifted the dog and set him in the truck, grunting as he did and saying, "See? He's following us."

"Christ on a crutch!" Ian moaned, climbing into the cab. "Come on, get in. But this one's yours to explain. I have enough problems."

With the three-legged dog settled between the two boys, they continued toward camp. Panting happily, the dog looked down the road ahead and responded warmly when Curt pet him.

"Wonder how he lost his leg," Curt said, inspecting the knobby stump where his right front leg had once been.

"Dodging trucks, probably. . . " Ian offered. "Hyatt won't let you keep him, you know."

"No, bear trap more likely," Curt continued, not hearing Ian's warning. "I don't think you like dogs, McKenzie. You haven't even petted him."

Ian looked over at the dog and imitated his lunatic, panting expression, whereupon the dog lapped his face.

"There! I let him french me. You happy?"

They entered the drive into camp and Ian said, "You

won't be able to keep that thing. You better not get too attached to him."

"We could hide him in Deerslayer until. . . "

"Sure, he'd just love being cooped up in a hot cabin. That dog's been chasing things all his life. You'd have better luck telling Hyatt he's trained to sniff out rock than to. . .

"Oh, a rock hound?" Curt asked blankly.

"Very funny. Look, Hyatt may not be the smartest man around, but letting you keep some stray mutt goes against every rule. Hell, even I know that." He slowed the truck and added, "Hop out and get the gate."

"Aw, Christ," Curt said.

"Quit gripping and get the friggin' gate," Ian barked.
"Ackerman."

Ian followed Curt's gaze. Ackerman was standing next to the gate, his cigarette, his stare, his usual accompaniment.

"Shit. Let me do the talking," Ian whispered to Curt.

twelve

When Ian jumped down out of the truck cab, his legs nearly buckled under him. It didn't seem as though he had worked much more than his brain that day, but as he walked 'round the truck he took a glance at the wonderful load of rock he had bargained for and realized his aches were not in vain. He approached Ackerman and asked, business-like, "You get my note?"

Ackerman pulled the gate open and replied, "Yeah, I got yer note."

Ian indicated the truck bed full of rock. "What d'you think? Not bad, eh? And there's plenty more where. . . "

But Ackerman wasn't admiring the rock. He walked to Ian, pulled him toward his face by his jacket, and said, "You coulda got us all kicked outa here, you son of a bitch!"

Ian, although not expecting Hail the Conquering Hero, did not expect violence, and he reacted in kind. "Let go a' me, you. . . " he said as he tried to push Ackerman away.

Curt had come round the truck to Ian's defense. He shouted, "Andy, he did it for you! He did it for you!"

Ackerman, still clenching Ian, arm ready to strike, paused as Curt's screaming words hit him. He slowly relaxed, let Ian go, and said to Curt, "Thought y'all'd cut out on me. . . "

Ian, recovering his dignity, feeling his heart pound in his chest, picked up his cap, set his jaw righteously, and said, "I put it in goddam writing, for Christ's sake!"

Ackerman seemed to slump some. He stepped back and repeated, "Thought y'all'd cut out. . . "

As though insulted to be left out of such drama, the dog stuck its head out of the truck window and barked at the trio.

Ian said on Curt's behalf, "Curt found a dog. He wants to keep him." But Ian was talking to Ackerman's back. The counselor approached the dog and gently pet him.

"Cain't," Ackerman said, stroking the dog. "Ain't no dogs allowed."

Curt, recognizing a fellow dog lover when he saw one, piped in with, "He's really a neat dog, Andy. Look, he only has three legs."

"Great, alls I need's another charity case," Ackerman mumbled as he looked the foundling over.

The dog spied a flock of seagulls on the lawn, barked wildly and, before anyone could advise him otherwise, leaped out of the window, making a perfect three-point landing. He was off chasing the seagulls, ignoring Curt's pleas to stop. Ackerman put his fingers to his mouth, gave a heart-stopping whistle, and the dog immediately returned.

Curt and Ian looked at each other, shrugged their shoulders, and watched Ackerman wrestling with the dog. "Well, I reckon ol' Harry cain't bitch if some critter jest wandered into camp all by its lonesome," Ackerman finally decreed.

Ian took the cigarettes from the cab and offered them down to Ackerman. "Here, I picked these up for you."

"Thought you didn't approve a' smokin'," Ackerman said, accepting the gift.

"I can take it or leave it."

"Much obliged," Ackerman said.

Ian noticed how pale Ackerman's skin was, how thin his lanky arms. Only a small, faded tattoo on his right wrist attested that he was a sailor . . . no tanned Popeye muscles or salt-weathered skin . . . no healing battle scars for explanation as to why he should be spending a summer at a boys camp rather than on the gun turret of a ship.

Ackerman, seeming to sense Ian's eyes upon him, rolled down his shirt sleeves past his elbows. Ian was embarrassed to have been caught staring.

"I wasn't going to cut out, you know," Ian said, kneeling now and petting the dog.

"You coulda ruint everything," Ackerman said softly, lighting a cigarette.

"But I didn't."

Curt approached them and, the worst apparently over, said, "Swell dog, eh?"

Ackerman looked at the dog fondly and replied, "A dog's a dog." He leaned back and closed his eyes on the sky above. The dog, quite content, put his head against Ackerman's leg.

Ian stood up and said to Curt, "Come on, Hollenbeck, let's get this rock unloaded."

Back in the truck, Curt looked at the dog and Ackerman lying on the grass. "I hope he knows that's *my* dog. Look at that Ackerman. You see his eyes? Think maybe he's drunk or something? For a minute there, I thought he was going to rip your head off."

Ian looked at Ackerman as he drove the truck up the service road and said, "Woulda been his last act on this earth."

They unloaded the rock in a neat pile close to the dining hall, returned the truck, and began trudging, beat-to-the-socks tired, up the path toward Deerslayer. A swim was needed, followed by food and sleep.

Curt saw them first and pulled Ian back by the sleeve, "Look! Wimmen! Oooo, firm and round and fully packed!"

Ian stopped and looked into the woods. There he saw an attractive woman, her teenaged daughter, most likely, and a man of the cloth. They stood quietly, heads down, almost as though visiting a grave site. Curt and Ian hid and watched a counselor come walking up to meet the gathering, his hand on the shoulder of one of the Roswell campers. Upon seeing his mother, the boy ran and they fell together in a tearful embrace. The daughter began crying and the minister followed them as they walked slowly back up the path toward the parking lot. The counselor simply stood and watched them disappear.

"What'ya figure that was all about?" Curt whispered to Ian from their spying spot.

"For crissakes, Hollenbeck, take a guess!" He pulled Curt away and added, "God, you're obtuse."

Curt stole a last glimpse of the family as they disappeared up the path and said quietly, "Oh, I guess the father checked out."

"Go to the head of the class, Hollenbeck."

Curt kept looking, and Ian pulled him along. "Come on, Curt, let's hit the water."

Curt turned slowly and said soberly, "Guess it could happen any time."

"You know, maybe we oughta enlist in the Western Union. That's where the *real* action is! Bereaved widows, thankful daughters and all. . . "

"That's a disgusting thing to say!"

"Lighten up, Hollenbeck! It's only a joke, for cryin' out loud." And Ian sped up, leaving Curt to his thoughts of war, fathers, Italy.

The dog, in no uncertain terms, had been delivered into an exalted state of nirvana. With a friendly boy at every breakneck turn, an endless supply of trees, and a waterfront that demanded constant seagull surveillance, he appeared to have every intention of making Roswell his home, with or without Hyatt's blessing.

Quite appropriately, he chose Deerslayer as his place to collapse and, as Ackerman had predicted, the dog found good company among the SOKs, their leader his own precious leader. In the cabin of misfits, the dog had found a sympathetic, appreciative home. And Ackerman had found a friend.

That evening, on the Deerslayer porch, they sat

watching the dog running in a dream, effortlessly, its three legs twitching in great chase.

"What are you going to name him?" Freddy asked.

"Hopalong!" G'Nat suggested with a laugh.

"I got a name for him," Ackerman said from his perch on the porch railing. He exhaled smoke rings into the night. "Yep, Kami*curz*i I reckon is the handle fer that mutt."

"Kamicurzi?" the boys echoed.

"What kind of a stupid name is that?" Ian asked.

Ackerman looked out into the night, took a long drag, and replied, "It's sort of a Jap word."

"Jap? Nothing doing!" Curt protested. "I'm not naming my dog after anything Jap!"

Ignoring him, Ackerman continued, "When yer sittin' on the deck of a ship an' it's all quiet . . . like it is now . . . you start thinkin' 'bout that Tokyo Rose talk."

"Tokeeeyo Rose?" Freddy jumped in, eyes suddenly wide and eager with war interest. "My dad dated her once. . . "

"Shut up," G'Nat said, listening to Ackerman.

"She'd tell us 'bout this thing called Kamikaze . . . Dee-vine Wind. She said fer us to keep watchin' the sky, cuz one a' them kamikazes jest might could be out there . . . it's a plane outa the sky, fulla dynamite . . . well, the pilot, he don't give a damn he dies. He jest crashes into the ship an' Wham! automatic entry through the Pearly Gates, or whatever the hell them Japs go through." He paused as the boys tried to visualize such a mission.

"A suicide mission! Man oh manoroony!" G'Nat said, looking out over the cove.

"Yep. 'Course I never seed one, but that don't mean

they ain't out there," Ackerman concluded. "Crazy Japs," he added with his mysterious half-smile. "That's what we oughta name that damn mutt. I reckon he's as nuts chasin' trucks as them Japs is chasin' eternity."

Curt rolled the strange word over and over out loud, and having been charmed by the dog's wild abandon and carefree, chaotic, suicidal nature, agreed on the name. Any dog that dashed in front of trucks as though on a personal bombing mission calling for death's honor would fit right in with the SOKs of Deerslayer.

Kamicurzi it was.

thirteen

It took two more days to load and unload the rock from the Christmas tree farm. On the last load, Ackerman delivered ten disgruntled boys to prune trees for the old woman and left them there for a good ten hours. All but the exhausted ten pruners seemed satisfied with the arrangement.

When the SOKs had unloaded the last truckload, Ian proudly noted how this latest acquisition added a definite improvement to the already giant pile of stones. Freddy and G'Nat had worked right alongside Curt and Ian and, finally, the five weary Deerslayers rested on their mountain to survey their next step.

The hole in the lodge that Ackerman and the younger boys had created for the fireplace bed stared back at them with glaring audacity. Dinner was being prepared inside the lodge, and the clanking sounds echoed through the orifice.

Ian, perched atop the rock pile, looked down on Ackerman and asked, quite simply, "Are you sure you know what we're doing?"

"I'd say it's a mite late fer ignorance, boy," he said back, stretching out on the grass and examining the lodge's high gable.

"When we gonna start building the damn thing?"

asked Freddy, sitting on the ground and rolling a small rock with his foot.

"Yeah, when's the fun-o-roony part?" G'Nat joined in, whining purposefully. He rolled his braced leg impatiently. The squeaking of the knee-joint in his leg brace accented his words.

"Y'all need some oilin', son," Ackerman said, leaning over to inspect the brace. "That leather could use some soapin' too. This here salt air'll dry that leather up like beef jerky, 'less y'all oil it."

"I don't need oil or soap, I need some fun!" G'Nat moaned.

"Y'all wanna quit?" Ackerman asked the membership.

"We just want to start *building*," Freddy explained on behalf of the others.

"Yeah, there's enough rock here to build a house, let alone a stupid fireplace," Curt added. "I suppose you're going to want us to take *back* the rock we don't use!" He threw a small rock for Kamicurzi to retrieve.

Ackerman rose, lit a cigarette, and let his lighter close with a resounding snap of authority. He walked around the rock pile in silent thought. Ian followed him with a doubtful expression, squinting out the glare of the late afternoon sun.

"Yup. Yup," Ackerman finally said, "I reckon it'll be enough rock, all right."

"Praise the Lord and pass the ceee-ment!" said Freddy, hands up in the air with a sacrilegious grovel backwards.

"But. . . " Ackerman continued.

"Oh no," Curt said, this time throwing a rock clean

into the cove below. The dog cascaded down the hill full tilt and dove fearlessly into the water after it.

"But what?" Ian demanded.

". . . there ain't one here anywheres," Ackerman said, still surveying the rock pile like a defeated naval commander counting the surviving ships of his returning armada.

"Ain't one what?" Ian asked, starting to feel an intense dislike for Ackerman's mood swings.

"We cain't start ceementin', men. Not jest yet. Ain't got us no cornerstone." Ackerman put out his cigarette with a determined stomp.

Ian jumped down off the pile to confront Ackerman. "Take your pick!" he shouted, pointing to the huge stone gathering.

"Ain't one there," Ackerman replied, shaking his head sadly.

"How stupid can you get?" Ian continued. "What do you mean, no cornerstone? Just pick a goddam rock and start!"

The other three boys watched Ackerman carefully as he withstood Ian's fire.

"Nope. Nope. Cain't start till we got us a proper cornerstone," he continued with an odd, determined smile.

Ian picked up the nearest rock and handed it forcefully to Ackerman. "Here! Here's your friggin' cornerstone!"

Ackerman turned the rock over carefully, then set it back down on the pile with most tender care. The boys became more uneasy; the tension in the air was brittle.

"Come on, Ian," Curt intervened, pulling his friend away from Ackerman.

"No, wait!" Ian growled. "Look, Ackerman, we've been bustin' our butts at this thing for almost two weeks. There's your rock! Can we just get on with it?"

No one knew what to expect out of Ackerman. Clearly, he had already demonstrated he wasn't to be trifled with, and yet no one had pushed him as far as Ian was now.

Fueled by Ackerman's silent hesitancy, Ian gathered more righteous wrath and took a step closer. Even Kamicurzi, wet, exhausted, and shivering, set down the retrieved rock and seemed to watch, as though realizing no one was going to throw anything until the confrontation was over.

Finally Ackerman replied, "Cornerstone's the most important rock a' all, son." He spoke softly and his face was now hard, unforgiving, unyielding. "The wrong cornerstone jest upsets the natural order a' things."

By Ackerman's voice and expression, Ian knew he was supremely disappointed that Ian had not understood the importance of cornerstones. Realizing that Ackerman was not a man of rational expectations, he said bitterly, "All right! So what's so goddam special about your cornerstone?"

"Well, it's the startin' point, don't cha' know? It's gotta be long an' kinda flat. An' its gotta have lotsa courage if'n we're askin' it to hold up all that," Ackerman explained, lighting another cigarette and studying his mountain.

G'Nat nudged Freddy to make sure he was watching Ackerman as carefully as *he* was.

"Courage? Yeah, right!" Ian challenged, his hands on his hips. He desperately wanted to look at Curt, but didn't dare take his eyes off of Ackerman.

"Gotta be at least two feet yea," Ackerman continued, demonstrating with his hands. He strolled to the gaping hole in the lodge, looked inside, then added, "Yes sir, that cornerstone's gotta have a whole lotta heart. Cain't start without it."

With their leader's back turned, Ian ventured a look a Curt, then down at the others.

"Now let me get this straight," Ian pursued, trying to anchor his sun-bleached eyebrows together to insure a more serious expression: "you want one cornerstone, two feet long and flat. It has to have courage and heart. Any particular color? Say, how about something in a gray fleck?"

Ackerman walked back over to him, leaned his head back, displaying his long neck and bouncing Adam's apple, and laughed. There was something very honest and very contagious about his drawling heh heh heh that made the others release little chuckles of relief.

"It can be blushin' pink with little yeller polka dots, fer all I care. Y'all jest git me that cornerstone an' I'll start buildin'," Ackerman said with congenially sliding words. As he passed Ian, he slapped him cordially on the back.

"You're full of bullshit!" Ian said as Ackerman passed.

No response.

"You're crazy, you know that, Ackerman?"

No response. Ackerman kept walking. The other SOKs looked at each other and wondered how far Ian would go. Ian looked at his cohorts, shrugged his shoulders, and called out even louder, "Well, we'll need the truck then!"

Ackerman simply waved his hand absently as he continued on up the path to Deerslayer.

Ian turned to the others, spit, and said, but only half-whimsically, "He is! He's a crazy son of a bitch. Gets crazier every day!"

"A rock with courage and heart?" Curt exploded, unable to contain his laughter.

Ian offered G'Nat a hand up to his feet and grumbled à la Ackerman, "Yessir, them's rare qual'ties in a rock."

fourteen

Dinner that evening was breezier than usual because the hole in the lodge sucked air through the huge room and also because, Ian noted, Hyatt's announcements were more long-winded than usual. He began by asking the boys not to encourage "that three-legged dog" and maybe it would go home. Ian looked over to his comrades, who had each already stashed a tidbit for the newest SOK.

Then Hyatt spoke eloquently on what wonderful work the men of Deerslayer were doing and how everyone could take a lesson from their fine sense of camp spirit and commitment. He talked about the project being much larger in scope than anyone had first imagined and how lucky Camp Roswell was to have Andy Ackerman's skills of supervision and masonry. Without any choking down of milk or a-lot-you-know snickers, the SOKs listened and accepted all of Hyatt's accolades. He finished by saying that, with God's good grace, by summer's end every Roswell boy would benefit from the hard work of the Deerslayers. An unforgettable ceremony of dedication, complete with barbecue, was being planned.

"And lastly. . . " Hyatt continued.

"No such thing," Ian whispered to Curt.

". . . don't you boys eat too much blackberry buckle," Hyatt said. "The boys of Longstocking and

Cherokee have challenged the boys of Mohawk and Deerslayer to a baseball game after dinner. If the challenge is accepted, the losers will make ice cream for everyone."

The boys of Mohawk looked across the dining room at their four unlikely teammates from Deerslayer and began griping among themselves at the unfairness of life.

"Get together after clean up, boys, and work out the details. Cabin counselors, as usual, are captains and umps. May the best team win," Hyatt continued, his tan face scowling in his best-attempted grin.

Ian mumbled to Curt as they stood in line to pass their plates through to the boys on K.P. "I thought we were immune from all this camp shit."

"It's only a stupid ball game. Besides, we can always bug out," Curt replied

"And have all those society boys think we're chicken shit?"

"Let's see about Freddy and G'Nat," Curt suggested, looking around for the two boys. "Where'd those twerps go?" He looked back to their table and saw that they had escaped without helping clear. "Those jerks."

Ian and Curt went out the back steps and ran around the lodge. When they saw Freddy and G'Nat walking the trail by the waterfront, Curt pulled Ian back by the shirt sleeve. It suddenly was obvious why the two younger SOKs had made their escape.

Before Curt or Ian could say anything, Ackerman spoke from behind them. In his perpetually casual drawl, he said, "Reckon they don't feel much like playin' no baseball."

"No, I reckon not," Curt said, watching G'Nat and Freddy limp and waddle along, two unto themselves.

Without saying a word, Ian ran until he caught up with the two. "Look," he said, out of breath, "the way I see it, the four of us are a team now. You know?"

"You and Curt go play baseball," Freddy said. "G'Nat and me'll watch."

"Yeah, it's okay, Ian. We'll watch," G'Nat concurred, but his small voice resounded with the hurt of yet another reminder of his infirmity.

"Bullshit you will!" Ian stopped and pulled each boy back by an arm. "All or nothing!"

Freddy and G'Nat searched each other for a verdict.

"Naw," Freddy, the consummate spokesman, said. "Go on ahead."

Curt caught up with them. "You guys playing?" he asked. "The Mohawks are waiting."

"Got an idea. . . " Ian said. His suddenly wide eyes and evil grin alerted the others.

"Oh mur-der," Freddy moaned, turning back toward the trail.

"No, wait. Why don't we accept the challenge, but with a few of our own rules," Ian continued.

"Like what?" G'Nat asked suspiciously.

"Haven't you guys ever played 'Anything Goes'?" Ian asked, as though it was the game that was all the rage. "That's it. We'll tell those guys we'll play 'Anything Goes.' Let's go talk to the Mohawks." He started off.

"What's 'Anything Goes'?" Freddy asked G'Nat.

G'Nat shrugged his tiny shoulders, contorted his face into a whimsical frown, and led, "If McKenzie plays it. . . "

"God only knows. . . " G'Nat and Freddy moaned in unison.

Within a short time, the challenge was accepted with Ian's provisos, which he outlined in the succinct detail: precisely, anything goes. They agreed on only two innings, this being a concession to the adults, who had shown some skepticism for Ian's rules.

The challengers christened themselves the Indians and the boys of Mohawk and Deerslayer coined themselves the Mad SOKs.

Ian took a glove and confidently tossed the ball into it as he talked to the leader of the opposing team. "So, the only rule is this: no rules."

"No rules at all?" he asked.

"Well, there is one unwritten rule.

"And what's that?

"My team wins," Ian replied, tossing the ball to him and turning his back.

"We'll see about that," the boy called out after him.

The Indians won the toss to bat first. Ackerman, although the official coach of the Mad SOKs, remained tentatively along the baseline. To keep him from taking the ball, Kamicurzi had been tied to a tree, and he moaned and whined and begged to be set free to join the game.

Before taking their field positions, Ian called his team and formed a football huddle. Curt agreed to pitch, and Ian insisted on catching, so that he could better call the game. They remained in their huddle quite some time, until the Indians objected to this obvious intimidation tactic. The vital tone for the game was set. Finally, the Mad SOKs distributed themselves in the field, and the game began with a reasonable semblance to the game of baseball.

That quickly ended. Curt's first pitch was accepted with an arrogant crack of the bat, and the hitter got to third base long before Freddy and his two fellow outfielders could retrieve the ball. He strolled home victoriously, grinning cockily at Ian as he passed home plate.

The next three hitters repeated the standard.

Pulling up his catcher's mask, Ian called, "Hold everything!" And he waved for his team to meet him in the huddle again.

Inside the huddle, Ian spoke gruffly. "We might as well change our names to the Chicken Shits," he began. "I don't think you guys quite have the rules down on this thing."

"I thought you said, weren't no rules!" one of the Mohawks hollered, as exasperated as the rest.

"Now you're getting it, Larry. How come you're letting those guys past second?"

"If I don't have the ball. . . " Larry said, looking around to his teammates.

"Look, men, the only way this works is to think diabolically. This isn't baseball, this is war. All is fair," Ian continued. He sketched out some plays in the dirt, ignoring protests from the other team. After some ego-bolstering cheers, the Mad SOKs finally took their positions with an evil yelp of team enthusiasm.

When Ian saw the next Indian coasting past third base and coming in for the fifth home run, he picked up home plate and, with a mighty sling, tossed it well into the woods behind them. The confusion that followed allowed time for the ball to come sailing in. Ian caught it, chased the befuddled runner, and tagged him out.

"Out!" the umpire screamed.

The Indians protested, but the ump, after calling for quiet, simply said, "You boys agreed to anything goes. Batter up!"

"But what about home plate?" another boy protested.

"You can't score a run without touching home plate," the ump said, pulling down his face mask. At that, the Indians all scrambled to retrieve home plate.

"Batter up!" the ump called again.

"Quick! Pitch!" Ian screamed to Curt.

Curt pitched a perfect ball directly over where home plate should be.

"Strike!" the ump called. But there was no batter up.

Curt pitched two more balls, more or less within a batter's strike zone.

"Out!" the ump called. "Batter up!" he called again dutifully.

"Three more, Curt! Quick!" Ian called. The Mad SOKs were cheering wildly and laughing as the frantic search for home plate was stirring up dust in the woods.

By the time home plate was found, relayed back, and slapped down, the Mad SOKs were coming in to bat.

"Hey! What gives?" one of the Indians asked.

"I just struck two of your men out," Curt said, handing the ball to their pitcher.

"But we were all in the woods!" he protested to the ump.

"Anything Goes!" the Mad SOKs sang.

Ian's hit, after two strikes, was honest and long. He

ran to first, reeled around second, and stopped at third. Curt stepped up to the plate and his first hit was an easy homer. He took off for first as fast as if his hit were only a short line drive. Ian raced for home and, stepping on it, kept going around toward first, following Curt's furious pace. Together they ran the bases.

"Throw home plate!" the pitcher screamed to his catcher.

But before the catcher could get his wits straightened out, Freddy, in all his overweight glory, had gone and stood firmly on home plate.

By the time the ball was found and tossed back to the infield, Ian and Curt had run the bases three times, bringing the score to Indians: four; Mad SOKs: seven.

Despite the Indians catching on to the strategies of the game, the Mad SOKs, in one illicit fashion or another, pyramided their score to twenty-six. The spectators, even the wary adults, were going wild with the antics, and by the time the Indians got up to bat again, the game had become an arena for theatrics and one-upsmanship. The Indians made a stunning comeback, stealing many of their opposition's tricks and inventing a few of their own. They took the field having brought their score to twenty-seven.

In their last huddle, Ian spoke solemnly of team pride and honor and glory and how the taste of winning could only be sweetened by the taste of ice cream made by their enslaved, conquered team.

"Two runs. That's all we need," he concluded. "Two measly runs. Who's up?"

"G'Nat," Freddy answered skeptically.

G'Nat, who had previously avoided going to bat

through the pinch-hit option, asked, "Same plan? You
know, gimp hitter?"

"Nope. You're hitting this time, kid. Nothing less
than a triple," Ian replied sternly.

"Yeah, sure, right-o-roony," G'Nat said sarcastically.

"Batter up!" the umpire called out.

"We're counting on you, Nathaniel," Ian said, for
the first time ever calling the boy by his proper name.

With the bat resting on his shoulder, G'Nat limped
up to the plate. His face was red and serious as he faced
the pitcher. The boys on both teams grew quiet. Even
Kamicurzi stopped barking.

The first pitch whizzed by him so fast, the bat never
got off his shoulder.

"Ball!" the ump called.

"Come on, y'all can do it!" Ackerman called from
the baseline, his first words of encouragement during the
entire game.

"Strike!"

"Eye on the ball," Ian chanted reverently. "Eye on
the ball. . . "

Now Kamicurzi was going wild from his tether.
Ackerman walked casually over to the animal, knelt next
to him and whispered, "You see what's goin' on here,
boy? See that ball? Reckon you want it more'n life itself."

Then quite to his own amazement, G'Nat made
contact with the ball on the third pitch. It was a hit so
weak, it looked like a bunt. But as soon as G'Nat had
dropped the bat, mostly out of shock, Ian went into
action. At the same time, Ackerman released the dog and
he sped out toward the ball.

Ian ran ahead of G'Nat, leaned down so that the

boy could leap aboard his back and, one hanging onto the other's neck, the two streaked for first base. At the same time, Curt ran toward the ball, snatching it away from the pitcher's glove. Then, for all he was worth, he threw the ball clear into the bushes beyond left field, commanding Kamicurzi to fetch it.

The catcher tackled home plate before Freddy could commandeer it and together they struggled for possession.

As the fielders chased the dog with the ball, Ian and G'Nat cruised the bases to the cheers of the crowd. The catcher began to run with home plate clutched to his chest in a death grip, followed in hot pursuit by the rest of the Mad SOKs. Larry the Mohawk tackled him with the finesse of a linebacker. Boys from both teams heaped upon the pile, resulting in a major battle for possession of home plate. Freddy pulled out from the mass of scrambling boys and ran with the plate with all his might to replace it in time for G'Nat and Ian.

Ian stepped on it, set G'Nat down, stepped aside of home plate and said, out of breath, "I tied it. You win it!"

With a victorious step, G'Nat jumped on the plate. The ump put little G'Nat's arm high into the air and like a prize fight referee, called out, "The winnna and champeen!"

The crowd went wild, and G'Nat was hoisted on Curt's shoulders. The Mad SOKs, following Curt and the game's hero, ran single file around the bases in a victory lap, chanting,

"Anything goes! Anything goes!"

fifteen

The bruises and minor scrapes were easily attended to and quickly forgotten, but, just as Ian had predicted, the taste of the fresh peach ice cream melted into the sweet taste of victory, and the luscious combination lingered well past lights-out. Curt passed around a quart of warm beer, and even its bitter taste could not wash away the savory memory.

"Y'all better hush up in there now an' git in some sack duty," Ackerman's velvet voice called gently from the porch of Deerslayer. "Y'all gotta big day tomorrow."

The cabin was dark and silent, with only the faint, moody glow of the porch light seeping in. Each Deerslayer was wide-eyed and staring at the ceiling. Outside, the only sound was the squeak of Ackerman's chair as he leaned back with his feet up on the porch rail, rocking slowly back, rocking slowly forward.

Then he started to hum. The tune was melancholy, not at all the way the boys of Deerslayer felt, and at first Ian didn't recognize it. Ackerman's voice was oddly uneven, unsteady. Then, as he listened closer, he recognized it as the same song Ackerman habitually hummed. He stumbled through some words, then when the chorus was more familiar to him, he crooned off key.

"And when she holds my hand . . . Da, da, da, daaaa, da, da, da, daaa . . . And then I understand. . . "

Freddy, in his bunk, weaving a lanyard by porch light, absently joined Ackerman, whispering sweetly, "Da, da, da, daaa, da, da, da, daaa. . . "

Ackerman's voice stilled when he heard Freddy's voice and his rocker ceased its comforting creak. Then slowly he resumed, "Her eyes afire, with one desire, not a heavenly kiss, could I resist."

To which G'Nat, his baseball of victory in his hands, looking absently at his leg brace hanging above his bunk, joined Freddy's gentle refrain, "Da, da, da, daaa, da, da, da, daaaa. . . "

"And then I dim the lights. . ." Ackerman continued, then awaited Freddy and G'Nat's, "Da, da, da, daaa, da, da, da, daaa."

"And then we kiss good night. . . "

Ian looked at his younger, lower bunkmates, then over his head to Curt, who was running his finger absently around the lip of the beer bottle. Then, barely audible, Curt joined the youngers . . . "Da, da, da, daaaa, da, da, da, daaaaa. . . "

Ackerman then improvised, "Do, dah, doe, de, doooooooh, dah, doe, de dooooooh, dah doe de doooooh. . . " He stopped, as though gathering voice, gathering courage, then sang out, "She takes me to ParAAAAAdise. . . "

Silence. Ian ventured a peek at Ackerman on the porch, but saw only his back in the chair, feet still up, bluish smoke from his cigarette lofting toward the cove.

"Y'all better git on to sleep now," he whispered. "Ya got a early piss call tomorrow. Yer gittin' me my cornerstone." With that, he rose, took the steps down with heavy footsteps, nearly missing the last step, and left.

As they often did, the two older boys waited for the younger ones to fall asleep. Finally, about an hour later, Curt asked into the darkness, "McKenzie? You asleep?"

"No. You?"

"No."

"Well? What?" Ian asked, punching some comfort into his flat pillow.

"Where we going to look for Ackerman's cornerstone?"

"Thought we'd head south this time," Ian said. He too had been thinking about their task. He rolled over on his stomach and looked at Curt.

"What's south?" Curt asked.

"Places we haven't been."

"Oh," Curt whispered wisely. "How far south?"

"San Francisco. How the hell should I know how far south? Until we find it, I guess." Ian paused, then realized why he hadn't been able to sleep. "You hungry?" he asked.

"Yeah, but I'm too tired to do anything about it," Curt answered. "Freddy's asleep. Swipe a marshmallow."

"I could really go for a sandwich."

"Kitchen's closed."

"Yeah, as though that ever stopped me," he whispered, slipping down from his bunk and rummaging in the darkness for his pants and shoes. "You coming?" he asked Curt in a loud, demanding whisper.

"No. I'm asleep."

"Coward."

He carefully opened the door and peaked outside for

the telltale glow of Ackerman's compulsory cigarette. Looking toward the water, he could see or hear no one. In fact, Ian thought it eerie that the sky was moonless and the air so warm and still. Picking his way carefully down the path to the lodge, he stopped every few steps or so to listen.

Flashing back on when he was seven or eight, he remembered pestering his mother until she told the members of his neighborhood clan that he was part Indian. A lie of course. With or without Indian blood, he'd always fancied himself able to become invisible . . . in and out of the shadows like any respectable Indian . . . take a few airborne steps, stop, listen, smell the air, his catlike eyes pierce the dark and see what no mere human can.

In this fashion, Ian crept down to the lodge. The kitchen door was, as he had suspected, locked. It would have been easy to force the door open, but Ian paused to consider his pride and what would happen should he get caught. Keeping true to his childhood's Indian, he walked around the lodge in thought, knowing there must be an easier way.

"You idiot!" he finally swore out loud when he approached the rock pile. Remembering the hole in the side of the lodge, Ian knew the adventure would be less of a challenge than he'd thought. He scoffed at the chair set inside the hole as though to actually forbid entrance.

From there it was easy. The kitchen was well lit by a light on a pole just outside the service entrance, and Ian went straight to work preparing a sandwich of gastronomical proportions . . . one didn't risk limb and very life for a dry peanut butter affair, he thought to himself as he layered bologna between thick slices of cheese.

Satisfied with his creation, he grabbed a quart bottle of milk from the cooler and began shaking it as he carefully picked his way through the dining room tables.

The dock was the best place to consume his feast, he decided. But hungry as he was, the sandwich was half gone by the time he reached the waterfront. He quickly finished it off and took a mighty slug of milk to wash down the last bite. He was considering going back to build another one when he heard an odd knocking sound.

He swallowed and held his breath to listen for it again. The sound was coming from further down the waterfront, and he carefully walked toward it. Something hitting wood, he thought. It was an odd sound, frightening and out of context, unlike anything Ian had ever heard before.

Again it came. He stopped and strained against the darkness to discern the exact whereabouts of the thudding. His heart pounded against his chest when he heard a moan.

"Oh God, not now. . . " a voice whimpered into the night, followed by more agonizing thuds.

Instinctively clutching the milk bottle, Ian ventured further, preparing to witness a murder. The boat shed, Ian decided. It was coming from the boat shed.

Thud. Thud.

All the trouble in town and a murder out at camp. Ignoring the reflex to flee and get help, he slowly, cautiously crept closer.

"Oh God, God, God," a man cried from inside the shed. A weak light bled through the open door and

Kamicurzi sat, trembling, outside the shed door, obediently frozen.

Ian stopped cold. It was Ackerman's voice crying out from inside the shed.

Thud. Thud. Thud.

Betraying every streetwise instinct, Ian carefully pushed the shed door open. He had been prepared to witness just about any horror except the one he found.

Barely lit by a lantern, Ackerman stood with his face to the shed wall, bashing his forehead into the unforgiving wood. Blood streaked down his ashen face, and his black hair was wet and matted.

"Andy?" Ian whispered weakly.

His forehead still against the wall, Ackerman slowly looked over and saw Ian standing in the shadows, holding the bottle of milk. Ackerman turned around and leaned against the wall for support. The milk bottle slipped out of Ian's hand and crashed to the floor. Kamicurzi, grateful for the human intervention, sniffed the milk, then cautiously licked up a few drops.

"What's the matter, boy?" Ackerman gasped. "Ain't you ever seed a man crush his skull before?" He spoke with utter exhaustion. His chest heaved as he tried to claim breaths.

"God, Ackerman, what're you doing?" Ian asked in an horrified whisper.

Ackerman took some deep breaths, tried to smile, then clutched the sides of his head and shrank to the ground in agony. He buried his head in his wadded-up jacket and muffled a scream more hideous than Ian had ever dared imagine. Kamicurzi, head and tail low, hopped toward him.

"I'll get Hyatt," Ian offered, turning.

"No," Ackerman pleaded with a whisper and an out-stretched arm.

Ian stopped, confused and sickened. "But look at you!"

Ackerman wiped his forehead with his jacket and looked up at Ian. His eyes, always so unreadable, were now filled with unspeakable suffering.

"You need help!" Ian insisted.

Ackerman leaned against the wall and once more tried to smile. "No, I'm all right, Eeeon. I jest had me a little headache."

"So you try to put your head through a wall?"

"It's better now. I jest wanna set here an' rest a spell." His breathing became less spasmodic, and the bleeding from his forehead slowed. "Git along to Deerslayer, boy. I'll be on up after I clean up a bit."

"And just pretend I didn't see this?" Ian demanded. "Why aren't you seeing a doctor if your head hurts that bad?"

"Yer sure as hell a mouthy little shit," Ackerman said, closing his eyes. "Then git on in here an' close that door. Think I want the whole goddam camp knowin' 'bout this?" As Ackerman's voice settled, Kamicurzi's ears relaxed and he sat wagging his tail tentatively on the shed floor. Ackerman carefully touched his forehead and assessed the depth of the abrasions. "I guess I done it to myself this time. Think that'll look like I walked into a door or something?"

Ian entered, closed the door, and held the lantern up higher. "Yeah, a revolving door," he concluded, trying not to keep the light from quivering in his trembling hand.

Ackerman looked up. His face had softened and some color had replaced the pallor in his cheeks. But when he smiled up at him, Ian could see the agony still spilling from his jade green eyes.

Ian, for all his cocky wit, all his toughness and resiliency, couldn't say anything. Even at his age, he knew he was looking directly into the eyes of a dying man. Finally, he sat down on the bench and asked softly, "Can't I. . . ?"

"Ain't nothin' you or anyone can. . . " Again he was seized. His eyes rolled back and he muffled his screams of agony once again.

"Andy!" Ian gasped, reaching out to help.

Andy held his arm up to hold the boy away. Slowly, he gained control, and the jacket came back down. "Guess maybe I do need yer help, boy," he whispered.

"What?"

Ackerman reached into his jacket pocket and pulled out a brown bottle of pills and a black leather case, and tossed them to Ian. "I'm sorta seein' two a' everything jest now," he said, almost apologetically.

Ian took the bottle and started to open it. "How many?" he asked.

"Ferget them pills, son. Open that there case," he said, weakly pointing with a shaking hand.

Ian picked up the case and opened it. There, shining up at him, nestled in a bed of green velvet, was a silver hypodermic needle and a vial.

"You ever shoot drugs, son?" Ackerman asked.

"No," Ian whispered.

"Good on you, but you gotta do me one now, boy."

"I can't . . . I . . . "

"Easy as pie, Eeeon. Pull that there hypo down to where it says ten. Stick the needle through that rubber top on the vial. Yep, that's right." He tried to focus his eyes on Ian's work. "See, ya gotta put in what you take out. Push the air in, then draw me out ten of that shit."

Ian fumbled with the syringe and vial. "Come on, boy, it ain't surgery. You can do it."

Ian held it up to the light and filled the hypo. "Like that?"

"That's good, son. Jest sorta let it fall in."

"What is this stuff?"

"They give me them pain pills for now, and that's morphine for later. God, it's later, boy, it's later," he said, now shaking uncontrollably, as though the mention of the word 'morphine' made him tremble with anticipation. He looked toward the ceiling, and tears ran down the side of his face.

"Morphine?" Ian asked. His heart leaped at the word.

"I tried, Eeeon. God, I tried not goin' to the needle. Look at me," he whispered, rolling up his sleeve and exposing his arm. "I made myself a junker."

Another gasp of pain. "There's cotton and alcohol in that case," he said. Ian poured a small amount of alcohol on a wad of cotton and handed it to Ackerman. Ackerman dabbed the injection site, gave Ian a pain-filled wink, and managed an ironic, "Cain't risk me an infection now, can I?"

Ian held the hypo to Ackerman. "Here," he said.

"Did ya git the air outa it? Flick it with yer fingers

some, like you was shootin' marbles. Then let a little out to make sure."

Ian held it up to the light and did as he was told. Ackerman watched as the tip of the needle formed a tiny bead. "That's enough, son. Don't waste it."

Ian offered it again to Ackerman, who was now stringing a piece of rope around his arm just above his elbow.

"Goes right in there. See that vein, jest stick it in and push the plunger, Eeeon," Ackerman whispered.

Ian's hands were trembling. "I can't," he said.

"Sure ya can. Hurry boy, God, please hurry. . . " His face once again contorted, and Ian did as he was told. It seemed to take forever to inject the morphine. Ian took deep breaths to quell the wave of nausea he felt as he watched the needle disappear into the vein. The hypo finally emptied, and Ian pulled the needle out. As he did, Ackerman whipped off the rope and waited. A small stream of blood limped down his arm and dropped onto the floor.

Ian sat back and watched the morphine work its horrible, blessed magic. Slowly, a muscle at a time, Ackerman's face relaxed. His eyes warmed as he dabbed the blood away from the injection site.

"You done good, boy. You done good," he whispered, taking longer, deeper breaths. Then he turned to Ian and said, "I reckon it's some kinda miracle I lasted this long." He paused, then exhaled heavily, as though he were smoking. He looked away and added, "Some fuckin' miracle, eh kid?" He patted his forehead with the sleeve of his jacket.

"Is this from what happened in the war?" Ian ventured.

Ackerman leaned back against the wall and stared at the ceiling. His eyes seemed to blur with tears, and he whispered, "I got me a piece of shrapnel in my head, son. Some sailors swipe silverware from the ward room fer their souvenirs. Not me. I gotta take me home part a' the ship." He looked over to Ian and pointed to his left forehead, rubbing it gently.

The blackness of his humor horrified Ian. "Why didn't they take it out?"

"After the shellin'," he began with deep, careful breaths, "we was bodies an' blood everywhere. I must a' looked like I was a goner, cuz they jest let me lie. Back stateside, by the time the docs took a peek, they said they couldn't do nothin'." He paused, looked across the room in a blank, absent stare, and then added, "I reckon they jest didn't wanna be the ones to kill me. Reckon they thought it'd be more merciful to let that goddam sliver a' metal work its own way in. Said they'd make me comfy as they could. Like hell I was gonna die lookin' up at four white walls and them homely army nurses!" He looked at Ian and asked, "You ever see an army nurse?" He contorted his face, made a thumbs down, and said, "Mud fences!"

He took a deep breath and went on. "I heard about this situation. Camp. Found me a doc who took pity and fixed me up." He indicated the black case. Ian noticed Ackerman's words were now smooth, slurring into each other. "Gave me all I need a' good ol' U. S. of A. general-issue morphine." Ackerman examined his arm as though it were someone else's, lifted the wad of cotton, and looked at the injection site. "I tried, Eeeon," he whispered, watching a tiny bead of blood form. "I hate dyin' on morphine's terms, but it sure as hell beats them nurses."

"But other doctors. . . "

Ackerman shook his head, cutting him off. "Thanks anyway, son. Look, Eeeon, this here's between you an' me, you understand? Not no one knows about this. Not Hyatt, not my momma, not no one."

"But if I had to. . . "

"Nope. Nope, I ain't gonna let it go that far no more, Eeeon," he said, almost like a child promising to be good. "I can keep things under control. I know I can. But. . . " His voice changed; it was now menacing: "I hear you whisperin' this to anyone . . . I see one look a' pity on anyone's face and yer a dead son of a bitch!"

Ian had no intention of disputing Ackerman's wish. He didn't even bristle at the death threat. He knew Ackerman meant every word of it, especially now as he spoke with slurred talk and unfocused eyes. From the very beginning, he never doubted Ackerman's dark side. But his horror cloaked itself as anger, and he demanded, "Well, then why the hell did you have to tell me?"

Ackerman looked at Ian, his face oddly changed in the low light of the lantern on the floor. "Shit. I thought you was tougher'n that, Eeeon."

Ian rose to leave, feeling the sudden need for fresh air, clearer thoughts, perhaps cold water to wake him from this nightmare.

As he rose, Ackerman called him back softly. "Eeeon?"

"What?" Ian couldn't look back down at him.

"If anyone had to know, I'm jest as glad it's you. Now git on up to Deerslayer and hit the snore rack. Toss me my gaspers, will ya'?"

Ian ran down the path as though the waterfront were pulling him. He jumped the rope of trespass and ran down the dock, his footsteps echoing across the night stillness of the cove. He stood on the edge of the dock, his heart racing, his eyes stinging with tears that no one in the last six years had been able to cause.

He took a deck chair, threw it into the water with a mighty swinging heave, and screamed out, "God. . . !" Next a stack of life jackets . . . "Damn you!" . . . Then, one after another, oars javelined out into the cove as far and as brutally as he could throw, and with each one he screamed out, "God . . . Damn . . . You . . . Ackerman!"

sixteen

Jerked awake by a family squabble among the crows in the firs overhead, Ian rolled over, looked out the window, and watched the shadows of the early August dawn bring the cove to life. Sleep had worked its magic, for his first thoughts were simple, childlike, almost happy. Then, as his eyes adjusted to the light, Ian remembered the boat shed, the lantern light, that sickening thud of something on wood, Ackerman's eyes, the silver flash of the hypodermic needle — and the helpless ache down inside came crashing back to life.

He looked down at Ackerman, asleep in his bunk. In the forgiving shadows of Deerslayer, in peaceful sleep, he looked like an overgrown camper himself, just another SOK sent out from Tacoma to straighten himself around . . . to give his sinful or meager life a look at the brighter side of things, to learn lessons of nature, play a little ball, learn to swim, escape the constant worry of the war.

He looked closer and studied Ackerman's forehead . . . red, swollen, and bandaged on the left temple. Even though he was the only SOK awake in the cabin, Ian felt uneasy staring at Ackerman's self-infliction. He felt his heart speed up as the memory of their encounter in the boat shed filled his mind. Ackerman's cries, the agony in his eyes, quieted and soothed by the rush of morphine.

Then the muffled shrill of Ackerman's alarm clock spilled out from under his pillow, and Ian fell back down, pretending to be asleep. Slowly, as though the piercing alarm was only a faraway annoyance, Ackerman's arm reached under his pillow and he turned off the violator. Ian listened to him stretch and yawn, then he heard him get out of bed.

By the creaking of the floor boards, Ian knew Ackerman was walking about. He heard the shaking of pills in a bottle. One eye now open, he watched Ackerman pop something into his mouth. He slowly walked past the bunks and pulled out a quart of beer from Curt's footlocker. He washed the pills down, then walked back over to the mirror. Without moving, Ian was able to watch Ackerman take a long look at his reflection. He took a most clinical interest in his forehead wounds, lifting the bandage to see just how deep the gashes were.

Finally, Ackerman started waking the other boys. When he got to Ian, Ian protested nicely. The very last thing he wanted Ackerman to know was that he'd been awake the entire time. Awake and watching.

"What happened to you?" Freddy asked, sitting on his bunk and looking up at Ackerman's head.

"When yer my height, y'all'll understand the hazards a' low hangin' branches," Ackerman answered blandly, looking directly at Ian.

"I'll never be as tall as you," Freddy said, pulling himself out of his bunk and standing in his shorts mid-cabin.

"Y'all don't know that," Ackerman continued as he

combed his hair. He caught Freddy's reflection in the mirror.

"Oh yes I do," Freddy continued matter-of-factly, leaning over to his footlocker and pulling out a few marshmallows. "See, you're an ectomorph and I'm an endomorph. Everyone in my family's an endomorph."

"Tell me another one while that one's still warm!" G'Nat said, pulling his pants on inside his covers. "Endomorph. No such thing!"

"There is so! I'm an endomorph, you gimp!"

"Liar. There's no such thing, Fatso!" G'Nat persisted.

"Sure there is," Curt said, breaking up the potential is-so-is-not debate. "It just means his family is a bunch of stumps."

"Very funny, asshole!" Freddy barked.

"Ever think maybe it's all those marshmallows stunting your growth?" Ian asked.

"Nah," Freddy replied, getting ready to show his expertise. "See, when you're an endomorph it doesn't matter what you eat. I'll always be short and fat.Actually, it takes a lot of pressure off a guy. So I just eat and enjoy it." Yet another marshmallow went into his mouth and he proceeded to get dressed, the picture of a contented endomorph.

"Y'all need to still the static, hurry on up an' be first down to the ptomaine domain so's ya kin git on yer way," Ackerman said, leaning down to tie his shoes. Ian noticed him pause as the blood rushed to his head, but he continued on, disguising the sudden pain. "I'll rustle up some picks an' shovels. Y'all might need some rope an' chains too."

"What for?" G'Nat asked, struggling with his leg brace.

Ackerman walked over to him, helped with the buckles, and replied, "Y'all didn't ferget, did ya?" He laced the heavy boot that anchored the brace, then took his comb and combed G'Nat's unruly hair.

"For his cornerstone, you dope," Freddy said, plopping a marshmallow on G'Nat's lap. "Let's go get some of that ptomaine. I'm starved." He pulled G'Nat to his feet and the two unlikely speedsters raced for the door.

Ackerman supplied the boys with all the necessities for their journey, their "quest," as he called it . . . food, some cash, gasoline ration coupons.

"No midnight requisitions now, ya hear? Don't take nothin' you cain't rightly explain," he warned as Ian pulled himself into the driver's seat. Then, to the younger boys in the truck's bed, he added, "An' y'all be careful. Hyatt warn't too keen on this idea, so's y'all best not disappoint him. Y'all wanna come on back out here next year, don't ya?" There was a satirical lilt to his voice.

"Oh sure," Freddy nodded over dramatically. "I'm going to start saving my pennies as soon as I get back home. If I *get* back home, that is. If I don't get *worked* to death, that is."

With Curt and Kamicurzi sharing the cab and the two younger boys in back, Ian started the engine. Ackerman reached through the window and said, "Take care a' my dog, now."

"He's *my* dog, you know," Curt said defensively. "*I* found him,"

Ian slipped the truck into gear, and Ackerman stepped back and added to Curt, "Come September he's yer dog. Till then he's mine."

Ian eased the truck down the service road. The two truck-bed passengers waved good-bye to Ackerman, but Ian just watched Ackerman grow smaller in the rear view mirror.

As he had threatened, Ian pointed the old truck south, following the road signs to Shelton and Olympia. After an hour of speeding and careening down dusty roads, they finally hit a highway that offered a smoother course.

"So, why're we going all the way to Olympia?" Curt finally asked.

"Why not?" Ian asked back.

"You know what'll happen if Hyatt finds out we've been all the way to Olympia?"

"Aw, stop worrying, Hollenbeck. You're getting more and more like a scaredy-cat little ol' lady every day."

"Yeah? Well, it so happens you make me nervous, McKenzie." Curt leaned back and stuck his right leg out the window.

"So what's wrong with doing a little sightseeing?" Ian asked. The dog had started to lean into him, and he shoved him aside.

"That's bullshit, McKenzie," Curt challenged casually. "You couldn't care less about Olympia. Ever stop to think what might happen to us if we got caught so far from camp?"

"Four Lost Campers Seek Help From Governor," Ian announced. "I told you, stop worrying."

At that moment, there was a knocking on the thick window in the back of the cab. Curt looked around and was facing Freddy, his light hair flying in the wind. His mouth was wide open and he was pointing a chubby finger into it.

"What's he want?" Ian asked, looking in the side view mirror.

"Either he's going to puke or he's hungry," Curt replied, looking over to Ian. Then they both replied with a logical nod, "He's hungry."

"What time is it?" Freddy screamed into the window.

Curt looked at his watch and replied loudly, "It's only eight-thirty. Keep your pants on."

"Look in the box and pass him out something to eat," Ian said with a tone of parental impatience. "I don't want his starving blue eyes staring at the back of my neck all day."

"Good ol' Ackerman," Curt said, pulling out a quart of beer. "Always thinking of us."

Curt pulled a church key out of his pocket and popped open the beer. Ian remarked, "My old man drank a lot of beer. They say that stuff can kill you if you drink enough of it."

Curt took a long, relished drink, burped, then said, "So can water, if you inhale it." He offered the bottle to Ian.

"No thanks. It's a little early."

Curt stared at Ian to study this change in his attitude toward beer. "What're you saying? I drink too much?" he demanded defensively. "It's only a swallow or two of beer."

"I know. I know. Take it easy," Ian said. He paused before asking, "Ever drink the hard stuff?"

"Sure, when I can get it. You trying to tell me you don't?"

Ian, regretting a confrontation with Curt about a few stupid gulps of beer, looked over to him, tried to look nonchalant, and replied, "Yeah. Sure. Whenever I can get it."

There was another desperate, violent knock on the window. Curt's hand disappeared into the box. He brought out an apple and showed it to Freddy.

"No!" Freddy screeched against the wind.

Then G'Nat's head popped up and he too declined the apple.

Curt dove in for another offering. This time he pulled up a sandwich wrapped in concealing layers of waxed paper.

They refused that as well.

When Curt's hand touched the familiar box, his face lit up. "Bingo!"

"What?" Ian asked.

"The Freddy Van Slyke staff of life!" he announced officially.

It was as though Freddy could smell the delicacy from the truck bed. He cheered Curt for the find and reached around for him to pass the marshmallows out the door window.

Curt turned to Ian and said, "You see? We all have our weaknesses." He took another slug of beer, then balanced the bottle on his knee as he looked down the road ahead.

They drove for nearly another hour before the country-side began to melt into the outskirts of Olympia.

They zoomed past an old graveyard, and it was as though all three, Curt, Ian, and Kamicurzi, spotted the potential at the same moment. Ian slammed on the brakes, whirled the truck around, to the protests of the truck-bed cargo, and pulled up in a thunder of dust in front of the old wrought-iron gate.

"Pioneer Cemetery," Ian read. "You thinking what I'm thinking?" he asked Curt.

Curt put down the beer bottle and replied carefully, "I think there's some kinda law against. . . "

But Ian was already out of the truck, Kamicurzi was running up the hillside of the decaying graveyard, and Freddy and G'Nat were warning Ian from the truck bed.

Curt ran up the hillside and joined Ian, glaring down at a flat gravestone announcing to anyone who cared that little Jenny had died after two sick weeks back in 1893.

"Think she'll miss it?" Ian asked, his voice not nearly so enthusiastic, now that he was standing on the child's grave.

"Count me out," Curt said. "You can't steal some little kid's headstone. It's sacrilegious or something."

Ian walked to another grave site and said, "Well, this ol' lady lived to be," he subtracted birth from death and continued, "Seventy-two. There. That better?"

But Curt had found another grave headed by a gravestone column five feet high by two wide. "Hey, how about this? This'll make Ackerman wet his pants. . . "

Ian walked over to it, ignoring the entreaties of superstitious warnings from Freddy and G'Nat. "To Our

Lord, We Commend William Kelly Stapp, Private First Class, U.S. Army, Born October 21, 1899, Died September 2, 1918. . . " He paused to wipe some moss away from the final inscription. "In the Service of His Country."

"Some cornerstone, huh?" Curt asked, setting down the beer bottle and trying to rock the column. But Ian pulled him back and said, "Maybe this wasn't such a good idea after all, Hollenbeck. Come on. Let's head to Olympia."

"*Now* who's the coward?" Curt asked back, pulling his arm away from Ian's grasp.

"Come on. I only did this for a joke, anyway." Ian started back down the hill. "Bring the beer," he added.

Curt looked down after Ian, shook his head, picked up the beer, and followed.

"About another half hour," Ian announced after driving some distance in silence. He pulled to a stop and signaled a left turn with his arm out the window.

"Until what?"

"Until we're on the steps of the Capitol, you dope. Why did you think we came all the way down here?"

"Hell if I know. I thought we were supposed to be looking for a rock!" Curt bristled. "And I thought *I'd* found it!"

"Somebody else was using that one, Hollenbeck. Besides, we're not looking for just *a* rock," Ian replied. "We're looking for *the* rock. The only way Ackerman's going to get some . . . hell, the only way any of us are going to get some peace is to get him that stupid cornerstone." Ian's face became cold and his eyes intense as he stared at the road ahead.

So intense was Ian's stare, that Curt thought there might have been something alarming in the road ahead. He followed Ian's eyes and asked, "What is it?"

"Nothing. Nothing. Look, I want to finish that goddam fireplace more than anyone. You know what a wacko Ackerman is about that stupid cornerstone of his. Well, we'll bring him back a cornerstone, all right!" He took a sharp right following a sign pointing to the Capitol Buildings.

"Maybe this beer is making me fuzzy, but what the hell does Olympia have to do with any of this?" Curt demanded.

The truck slowed and then Ian pulled it to a stop directly across the street from the park-like entrance to the many legislative buildings, many of which were built of large rectangular stones.

Curt's face became solemn as he watched Ian look over the complex. "Ian?" he asked fearfully, his voice cracking involuntarily.

Without looking at Curt, Ian opened the door, stood on the running board, and said with a challenging smile, "Well, it's here someplace!"

seventeen

The other boys climbed out, stood on the grass, and looked around. As soon as Kamicurzi's long, thin nose hit the ground, he was off and running through the landscaped complex. Before Curt could entice him back, he had developed a personal relationship with every tree, bush, and fence post.

"Look at that," Curt said with paternal pride. "Ever see another dog pee standing on two legs?"

"Where is everybody?" G'Nat asked, doing a slow turn around the place. "I thought this was the capital."

"It is," Freddy said with his usual dour skepticism, "but this is summer. No politician works in the summer. Don't you know anything?"

"Oh," G'Nat replied logically, "I thought maybe they evacuated onaccounta the Japs might bomb the place."

"How stupid can you get!" Freddy moaned, looking very much like a miniature Oliver Hardy.

Then, as though he sensed G'Nat's dented pride, Curt said, "I don't think that's so stupid, Freddy. This place would be prime to some Jap-Kamikaze who just finished leveling McChord or the Bremerton Shipyards."

"Shit," Freddy said, a new sense of terror on his rotund face. "You think that could actually happen?"

"Sure," Ian concurred, adding powder to Curt's arsenal. "Every port on the west coast is a target."

"I didn't know that," Freddy added softly, his face growing pale.

"Why the hell you think we had all those blackouts early on?" Curt asked.

Freddy's face again was a tangle of new, confused lines. "My folks said it was to save electricity."

Ian, laughing with Curt, said, "Well, now we know where he gets his lying." Then he asked Freddy, "You *did* know there was a war on, didn't you?"

"Hey, lay off! My folks just aren't alarmists, that's all!" Freddy said, his ruddy face becoming even ruddier as it tinged with embarrassment.

Ian chucked one of Freddy's chins and said in a baby voice, "You mean, mommy and daddy endomorph don't wanna upset der wittle baby endomorph."

"Knock it off!" Freddy said, retreating. "At least they care enough about me to . . . to care about me!"

Ian laughed heartily and said, "You'll have to dig a hell of a lot deeper than that to get under my skin, Frederick."

G'Nat sat down on the grass and said, almost to himself, "Why are you making such a big deal out of this? I take back my damn question." Kamicurzi seemed to agree, and sat down next to him for moral support.

"Oh, I can dig deeper all right," Freddy challenged, facing Ian defiantly.

"Come on, you guys," Curt said. "I can't believe we've been in that truck for three hours just to. . . "

"No, wait. Go ahead, Freddy, dig deeper," Ian said, taking his street stance of hands-on-hip daring. "I dare you."

"Tell us about that scar on your neck!" Freddy said, pointing to Ian's throat.

Knowing perfectly well that was what Freddy would aim for, Ian simply answered, "Street fight. Just defending my territory. Some asshole pulled a knife."

"This is stupid," G'Nat exhaled to Kamicurzi, lying down and looking at the sky rather than the brewing confrontation.

"Well, I heard different!" Freddy said, keeping a careful distance yet pressing his words.

"Then you heard a lie!"

"I heard your old lady's pimp tried to kill you!" Freddy blurted out, as though he'd held this secret in all too long.

There was no power on earth that could have restrained Ian. He leaped for Freddy's legs and tackled him, bringing him down squarely. Before Freddy could even react, Ian was straddling his chest, gripping him by his collar, and threatening him with his right fist.

"You tell me what son of a bitch told you that," he spit, his blue eyes raging with white fire.

Displaying more street sense than Ian had given him credit for, Freddy relented rather than attempting a suicidal struggle. "It's all over camp, McKenzie! I'm sorry, I'm sorry," Freddy said, tears beginning to form in his tiny blue eyes.

Ian slowly loosened his grip and stood up. He knew he was supposed to deny it, but was unable to speak. It seemed as though his reputation and the gossip that spread from it had indeed preceded him out to camp.

"Hey, McKenzie," Curt said, "most of the guys think it's kind of neat."

"What? That my goddam mother screws any uniform above a private that passes through town?" In the past few weeks at camp, he had almost forgotten the hatred he felt toward his mother, the fight that had finally landed him in jail, the scar on his neck.

"No, that you were defending her," Curt said, offering Ian the easiest way out.

"Like hell I was." He looked at each comrade and added coldly, "I was saving my own ass."

He reached down and offered Freddy a hand. With a great heave, he pulled him up and asked, "You all right, punk?"

"Yeah. I guess."

"I take back my question!" G'Nat bellowed from behind them. "I take back my goddam question!"

With the confrontation over, the tension simply evaporated into the warm August day, and the SOKs quickly agreed that food was necessary if their mission was to go one step further.

They ate their pre-lunch snack on the lawn in front of the Capitol Building, a beautiful compliment to the nation's Capitol, with graceful steps terracing up to the main entrance. Leaning against the Keep Off the Grass sign, Ian picked up the pile he'd made of peanut shells and tossed the handful into the box.

"Well," he said, looking around the complex, "I suggest we break into pairs."

Freddy looked into the box and said, shaking his head, "We don't have pears. Only apples. Who wants an app. . . " He looked up and saw the other three staring at him with amused disbelief. He popped the last fragment of a sandwich into his mouth and asked with an insulted air, "What're *you* staring at?"

Ian rolled his eyes to the heavens and said, "I mean, two of us go this way and two of us go that way. You know, like posses in Westerns?" He illustrated with his hands and fingers as though talking to a deaf three-year-old.

"What for?" Freddy asked, shrugging his shoulders.

"Because we have to leave here no later than one o'clock in order to get back to camp by four," Ian continued, getting up. "That only gives us a couple of hours. Come on, you guys, we've got to get moving."

Two went east and two went west. They agreed to circle the complex in search of the cornerstone . . . a stone that, in addition to having the virtuous qualities Ackerman had specified, also had to be stealable.

Kamicurzi was the first to spot it and, with his healthy, inexhaustible supply, he marked it as his territory. Curt and G'Nat found him sniffing the rock and confirmed the find. Everything about it was right. It was the end section of a wall around a set of basement steps. It had rounded, imperfect corners, and the mortar holding it had been chipped away — maybe by the mason himself who, in standing back to examine his work, had second thoughts about this stone, its placement, its color, its quality. But whether or not it belonged there, it was a beauty — creamy gray with black flecks. Unlike the others around it, which were almost flawlessly white. The stone belonged to the SOKs as surely as the SOKs belonged to Ackerman.

G'Nat took a pencil and marked it with a large X,

then jumped aboard Curt's back. With a quiet victory yelp, they went back out into the complex to find Ian and Freddy. Just as they turned the corner of the building, they saw them and quickened their pace.

Watching them approach, with G'Nat clinging to Curt's neck and with the three-legged dog leaping joyously at their side, Ian had to laugh. "You guys look like an ad for Boys' Town!" he said, shaking his head.

"We found it!" Curt said, setting G'Nat down and trying to catch his breath.

"You found Boys' Town?" Freddy asked automatically.

"You won't believe it. It's perfect!" G'Nat chimed in, ignoring Freddy. "Kamicurzi peed a 'C' right on it! Swear to God!"

"Hey, *I'll* do the lying around here," Freddy said.

"Come and see for yourself if you don't believe me!" G'Nat snapped back.

The four boys strolled casually around to the side of the building.

"Where?" Ian asked.

Curt waited for some men to walk by, then walked over to the three-foot-high wall of rectangular stones. "That one there," he said, pointing to a stone on the top.

Ian carefully looked around the area. The side of the building was well treed, and it was only a few yards from a quiet street. Then he closely examined the rock. The entire section of wall seemed to be crumbling into the stairwell below.

Looking over the edge to the basement entrance, Ian said, "Look at the junk down there. I doubt anyone even uses this entrance." He looked to his fellow Deerslayers and announced, "It's perfect! Son of a bitch! How perfect can you get!"

"And the beauty part is the mortar's all coming out!" G'Nat chimed enthusiastically while pulling a large chunk of ancient mortar from the wall.

"No, I'll tell you the beauty part!" Curt said, taking the piece of mortar from G'Nat and tossing it for Kamicurzi. "This joint ain't even open!"

"That thing must weigh a ton. How're we going to get it out?" Freddy asked, taking a serious, engineer's look at the chosen stone.

Ian called his comrades in closer and said solemnly, "Men, God is smiling on us. G'Nat, we need a lookout. Take the dog and hang around the front of the building. If anyone heads this way, throw a rock around back and the dog'll warn us off. Freddy, you and Curt start chipping away at that mortar. I'll bring the truck around with the tools."

"Who died and left you in charge?" Freddy demanded.

"*You* wanna bring the truck around?" Ian challenged back.

To which Freddy answered a meek, "No. I'll chip, I'll chip."

Ian began walking away. He turned and looked at the building, old, useless in war. Then he saw Curt and Freddy, allies, working around the cornerstone and said aloud, "Son-of-a-bitch perfect."

eighteen

Ian parked the truck as close as he could to the building. Then he assessed the distance they would have to drag the stone.

Curt came over to pull the tools and a tarp out of the truck and, following Ian's gaze, said, "So near, yet so far, huh?"

"How's it going?" Ian asked, helping Curt with the tools.

"Getting it out isn't the problem. Moving it's the problem," Curt said.

"Getting caught's the problem," Freddy grumbled, rummaging around in the box of food.

"Work now, eat later," Curt ordered, taking the sandwich out of Freddy's plump hand. "Come on."

Prying, drilling, and chipping as quietly and as fast as they could, the boys worked for a solid hour . . . three on the rock, with Freddy and G'Nat taking turns on the lookout. The SOK on guard would play casually in front of the building, throwing a rock for the tireless Kamicurzi. It was understood that Ian would do the talking if an adult came snooping.

When it appeared that the cornerstone was loosened on all three sides, they stood back to analyze their next step.

"Okay, each of us takes a grip and we'll see if she moves," Curt said, clasping his hands on the far edge and anchoring his feet against the bottom stone.

The other two complied, and on the count of three they gave a mighty, concerted pull. It didn't give the slightest indication of moving. Again. No luck. Again.

"You guys recall Ackerman saying the rock had to be stubborn?" Ian asked, his face reddening as he pulled with all his strength.

"Forget it, McKenzie. That thing ain't ever gonna move," Curt said, wiping the sweat off his forehead with a dirty hand. "What we need's a good, ol' fashioned, San Francisco earthquake."

"No, what we need is horsepower," Ian said, looking over his shoulder to the truck. "And there's some right there."

"Come on, Ian," Freddy complained, leaning back and rubbing his shoulder. "Even if we do get it out of the wall, how the hell we gonna get it up into the damn truck?"

Curt looked to Ian for an answer. Ian stared at the stone as if the answer were to be found etched into its beautiful granite surface.

"Worry about that once it's out of the wall," Ian said. "And you can kiss off the idea of me giving up now, if that's what you're thinking, Freddy. I'm taking this goddam rock back if I have to teach it to walk there! Come on, we're using the truck."

He pulled the chain and long coils of rope out of the truck. And while Curt went to work fastening the chain around the stone, Ian backed the truck onto the grass, being careful not to get too close to the giant alder next to the stairwell. Then Freddy tied the rope to the bumper of the truck.

"Think this old rope'll hold?" Freddy asked, pulling against the intricate knot he had fashioned.

"Well, it has to," Ian replied with stubborn resolve. "You tell me when she's just about to give way," he instructed, climbing back into the truck. "And watch your feet. That's all we need, another gimp," he added under his breath.

He lightly touched the gas pedal, and there was no forward movement. The old rope groaned against the strain and the chain snapped taut.

"Keep going," Curt said.

The ground under the wheels began to spin up dirt at Curt and Freddy, but despite the soddy shower, they held their ground.

"More. Easy!" Curt said. "It's coming! Once more, just a little!" Slowly, and under the protest of ages, the grand stone pulled away from its resting place.

Ian eased the truck out a few inches farther, and the rock finally tripped out and landed on its side. "Stop!" Curt commanded. "It's out!"

Ian killed the engine and ran over to inspect their work. Free of its confinement, the stone was even better than he had imagined.

"Ain't she a beauty," G'Nat said, holding Kamicurzi's rock in his small hand while the dog, panting frantically, stared at it desperately.

"Yeah," Freddy said. Then, seeing G'Nat, he demanded, "What are you doing here? You're supposed to be on lookout!"

"I'm tired of throwing this stupid rock for this

stupid dog," he complained. "*You* be the stupid look out." He placed the rock in Freddy's hand, bringing the dog to yelps of delight that a new machine was about to go into rock-throwing action.

"*Somebody* get him away from here!" Ian ordered. "Hurry!"

Freddy did as he was told, throwing the rock as far in front of him as he could.

G'Nat walked around the stone, then asked, "So why're you guys just standing around staring at that thing?"

"You know, you're right, G'Nat," said Ian, "let's get the hell out of here. Say, you mind picking that up and tossing it into the truck for us, Superman? Curt'n me're a little tired."

"Oh." G'Nat looked down at the rock thoughtfully, then added, "Well, maybe if we all pushed, we could roll it."

"That'll get it *to* the truck, not *in* the truck," Curt said.

"Oh." He limped over to the alder tree and sat down, leaning against the trunk. He looked up, saw the thickness of the branches, and a light of brilliance came over his small face. "You guyyyyyyys. . . " he called melodically.

"We can't plaaaaaay nowwwwwww," Curt replied in the same tune.

"But I have the annnnnnswerrrrr," G'Nat insisted, still staring into the trees.

The older boys looked over at him, then followed his gaze up. There, almost directly above the truck's bed, was a large, accommodating branch.

"Why didn't *you* think of that?" Curt asked Ian, hitting him playfully.

"Shit, I can't think of everything," Ian said, helping Curt work the chain back around the cornerstone. When they were satisfied the cradle of chain would hold, they tossed the rope toward the tree branch. It took several tries, but Curt finally hurled the rope up and over the branch.

"G'Nat, go get Freddy. We're going to need every pound of him," Curt said.

With the rope over the branch, the three larger boys each took a position on the end, tug-of-war fashion.

"What do *I* do?" G'Nat asked sarcastically. "Be the anchor man?"

Testing the weight and the tension of the rope, Ian replied, "G'Nat, you get into the truck and when we tell you, back 'er up till she's under the rock. Got it?"

"Me? Drive the truck? I can't even reach the pedals," he complained.

"You mean you never stole a car before?" Ian asked, shaking his head sadly, "And you call yourself a juvenile delinquent."

"I ain't a juvenile delinquent!" G'Nat said defensively. "Just a 'potential' juvenile delinquent!"

Wrapping the rope around his hands for a tighter grip, Ian continued to G'Nat, "Well, son, today you achieve your potential. . . "

Curt wheeled Ian around and said impatiently, "Do you think now's a good time to discuss potential, McKenzie?" He turned to G'Nat and said gently, "Look, there's nothing to driving." He quickly stuffed jackets and an old blanket behind him to prop G'Nat closer to the wheel. He was nearly prone and in no way could even see over the steering wheel.

"I can't see," G'Nat complained.

"You don't need to. Just do what I tell you."

Then Curt placed the boy's braced right leg onto the gas pedal, quickly explained what to do, then returned to his position on the rope.

"He'll be fine," he said to the others, but his face was less than confident.

"At least that clutch is loose," Ian said, wrapping the rope around his hands for a tighter grip.

On steady counts, they pulled back, and slowly the stone began to rise off the ground. It tipped and swayed and objected to the grip of the chains. By the time it was five feet off the ground, it began to sway like a deadly pendulum, making a steady tug more difficult.

"Christ, this better hold!" Curt groaned through gritting teeth.

"My balls better hold!" Freddy countered, leaning back against the rope.

"Hold your balls later," Ian said, feeling the rope burn through his palms. "Come on, you cupcakes, pull!"

The stone rose another hesitant few inches.

"Okay G'Nat! Bring her back *slow*ly," Curt ordered.

G'Nat crunched it into gear and, revving the engine, popped the clutch until the truck leaped backward a few feet, then died with a shiver.

"I can't hold this much longer," Freddy warned through clenching teeth, his face turning purple.

G'Nat tried frantically to start the engine again.

"Here, back around the tree trunk," Curt said, guiding them around. They were able to get a little relief by pulling the rope against the tree.

Knowing that the boys were in a game of some new, rare adventure, Kamicurzi began barking incessantly at them.

"Shut that goddam dog up, will you?" Ian spit to Curt over his shoulder.

"What do you want me to do, throw something?" Curt snapped back.

"He's going to flood the engine," Ian warned, feeling his strength give out.

With Kamicurzi barking wildly to be asked into the game, Freddy kicked up the trailing end of the rope. Gratefully, the dog accepted the invitation and, likewise, began pulling.

Finally, the engine started and G'Nat once again went through the steps to back the truck up.

"*Slow*ly. Let the clutch out *slow*-a-roony!" Curt called out.

"I'm losing it. . . " Freddy warned.

There was a tremendous screech as the truck felt its gears being stripped. But, slowly, it started to ease back just far enough when G'Nat killed it again.

"That's all! That's great!" Ian shouted. The rope was beginning to cut into the bark of the tree, and with the strain there was an odd smell of distressed, burning rope. "Okay, easy . . . *slow*ly . . . back around . . . the . . . tree. Lean back, Freddy! Just drop her easy . . . easy . . . that's. . . "

The rope broke with such a tremendous snap that the three boys lost their footing and fell all over each other.

The crash the stone made as it hit the bed of the truck was deafening.

All four boys scrambled to the truck bed to see what horrors the crash had caused, and how many pieces the magnificent stone had broken into. But there, lying squarely in the middle of the bed, wrapped in chain, the broken rope piled around it, was the cornerstone . . . in perfect condition.

They looked at each other with wide-eyed, Spanky-and-Alfalfa disbelief, shrugged their shoulders, and smiled at each other as though they had planned it — all along — to happen just this way.

They wrapped the tarp around their treasure and anchored it with their tools. Promising they would stop for lunch when they were well out of town, they climbed aboard the Camp Roswell truck and eased away from their pillage place.

Curt looked behind them at the huge gaping hole in the wall, their tire tracks leading away, and the dirt and grass splattered on the side of the building. "Think anyone'll notice?" he quipped.

Ian looked in the rearview mirror as he carefully eased the truck down off the curb. "Politicians? Naaahhh."

nineteen

They could have been carrying the Holy Grail back to King Arthur for all their vainglorious talk and smug, self-adoring smiles.

The four SOKs from Deerslayer ate their lunch in the bed of the truck, with their magnificent prize as their centerpiece. They took an oath on each other's lives that they would never tell where they got it. It had been their mission and it would be their secret. Forever.

The drive back in the hot August sun induced the younger boys to sleep in the truck bed, and soon Ian lost Curt to the gentle hum of the engine. Even Kamicurzi, normally alert and awake to help navigate the road ahead, slept soundly, his head in Curt's lap.

To keep himself from drowsiness, Ian began humming tunes and carrying on victorious conversations with past and future enemies. Eventually, his thoughts found their way to the War, as they usually had the last couple years. Since he'd come to Camp Roswell, he heard precious little about how the U.S. was doing in Europe and the Pacific. D-Day, June 6th, had changed just about every European point of view, but he'd heard little since that glorious day. He knew the camp counselors listened to the radio every night in the administration building, but as far as the campers were concerned, there wasn't supposed to be war anywhere in the world.

With things coming to a close in Europe, Ian turned his thoughts to the Pacific, the Japs, the Navy. He prayed the war would go on long enough for him to enlist . . . the perfect ticket out of town. Yes, the Navy. He looked great in white because he tanned so nicely. What the hell, he thought, even if the war was over by the time he turned seventeen, he'd enlist anyway. Nothing in Tacoma to keep him around.

He arranged the rearview mirror so he could take a clearer look at himself. Leaning forward, he concurred that his tan that summer was extraordinary, offsetting his blue eyes so much that they were almost eerie in their cool lightness. He looked at his cheeks for signs of a beard, but he was as smooth-faced as Freddy. He bared his teeth and assessed their straightness. And he was getting taller. He was coming along nicely, he decided. Solid. Maybe this fall, girls would take some notice.

When the road became blurry, Ian gave Curt a shove, saying, "Rise an' shine, Hollenbeck. Nap time's over."

Curt grumbled, "Knock it off," then wrapped his arms around his chest and slumped deeper into the seat.

"Come on, I'm falling asleep here. Keep me company." He pulled him away from the door to wake him.

"Shit and I was just about to get screwed, blewed, and tattooed," Curt protested, falling back against the door.

"I'm hungry. Anything left to eat? Hollenbeck!"

"I'm awake, I'm awake. What?" he asked, his face wrinkled from his sound sleep.

"What's left to eat?"

"I don't know. They have the box back there," Curt said.

"Well, ask them!" Ian said.

Curt looked through the window, then replied, "They're asleep. Why don't you pull over and I'll grab the grub."

"I don't want to stop. Climb back there and pass something up," Ian said as simply as though he were asking Curt to stroll to the kitchen for a glass of water.

"Screw that."

"You know, Hollenbeck, you haven't done one truly courageous thing since I met you," Ian baited, giving his passenger a serious glance.

"Who the hell cares? That's suicide." He motioned to the back of the truck. "You could die of hunger before I'd risk a stunt like that."

"Then send the dog," Ian suggested. "He's suicidal."

"Oh sure." Curt snapped.

"Cowards! Both of you!" Ian said, trying to maintain the decorum of a frontline general.

Curt leaned over, pointed a warning finger at Ian, and growled, "You call me a coward, you die!"

Ian looked at the tip of Curt's finger, leaned away dramatically, and said in his best Bogart, "Jeesh, I didn't think you'd have the moxshi to pull a finger on me. I like your shtyll, kiddo. You can join up wid me any time."

They stared at each other, wondering who was joking.

Ian finally said, a small smile coming to his face, "I'd stare you down, but I'm driving."

So, instead of staring they laughed and, for the remainder of the journey, talked about girls, gangster movies and, of course, the War.

Ian parked the truck just outside the entrance to Camp Roswell, and the four boys passed around the remainder of the beer. Curt had to hang on to Kamicurzi with two hands to keep the dog from retrieving the bottle after they threw it deep into the woods.

They planned their presentation to Ackerman. They would back the truck up, keeping the cornerstone veiled by the tarp. Then they'd place Ackerman atop the rock-pile, say a few lines; with great formal to-do, they would unveil the find and bask in Ackerman's drawling praise and, no doubt, dwell in the House of the Lord, forever.

"Amen," Ian said, with a sacrilegious roll of his eyes toward the heavens.

They climbed back into the truck and drove slowly, carefully up the service road into camp.

Ackerman, without any SOKs to supervise, was out in the middle of the cove, floating languidly about in a canoe. While Freddy and G'Nat called him in, Curt and Ian unloaded their supplies from the truck, then draped the entire truck bed with the tarp to make the unveiling more appropriately dramatic.

When they saw Ackerman being pulled up the path by Freddy and G'Nat, Ian and Curt took their positions on either side of the truck.

As planned, they sat him royally atop the rock pile.

Getting comfortable on his rockery throne, Ackerman sat perched with his long arms wrapped around his knees. His stubby cigarette was clinging to his lips, which Ian watched carefully for the sign of a smile.

"We, the Deerslayers," Ian began, speaking officially, "sometimes known as SOKs and other times known as rockseekers extraordinary. . . "

". . . no job too small. . . ," G'Nat piped, stepping forward and pointing to himself.

". . . no job too big. . . ," Freddy said immediately following, hardly able to keep a straight face.

". . . do hereby wish to present to you, Ackerman, King of the Deerslayers, sometimes known as Ackerman the Aggravated, this token of our esteem."

Curt, on the opposite side, stood grinning at Ackerman, but had clearly forgotten his cue.

Stepping out of character, Ian looked over to him and shouted, "Hey, Hollenbeck! You only have one line in this!"

Curt looked at Ian, startled, then looked over to Ackerman and recited, "We hunted and dug all 'round the clock, till finally we found it."

Then the four in unison, "So here's your damn rock!"

Each boy then took a corner of the tarp and slowly walked forward . . . pause, step, pause, step. Inch by inch, the cornerstone was revealed. The boys kept watch on Ackerman's face. By the time the prize was totally exposed, his face had gone virtually blank with astonishment. Ackerman stood up and, for the first time Ian had ever noticed, let his cigarette drop from his fingers.

The boys ran back to the bed of the truck, faces

alight with pride. Ackerman picked his way down the rock pile and walked to the cornerstone as though it were indeed the Holy Grail surrendered unto him.

He ran his hands over it with trembling tenderness, studying its magnificence.

Ian's heart raced with the excitement of the moment . . . how strange that one huge piece of cold stone could produce such awe on the face of a man and, at the same time, produce such a feeling of accomplishment in himself. Ian looked at Ackerman again. In the shadows of the late afternoon, his face appeared drawn and sallow. Blood had come through the bandage on his forehead and Ian noticed how his long, delicate fingers shook as he lightly touched the cornerstone, inspecting its perfection, like a blind person touching a surface in order to see it.

Unable to contain himself, G'Nat sparked with, "Well, what d'you think?"

"Don't . . . know . . . what to say," he began, his voice softer than usual. He looked at Ian and asked, "How in hell d'y'all. . . ?"

Not comfortable accepting praise, Ian shifted his weight casually and answered, "It just sort of fell into our laps."

"Oh sure, McKenzie!" Freddy barked, then added. "I think I got a hernia getting it outa. . . " Freddy stopped when Ian kicked him.

"So, what d'you think?" G'Nat asked again, his face full of Christmas.

"Yeah?" Freddy joined eagerly. "What d'you think, Andy?"

Ackerman looked down at G'Nat, ran his hand gently down his face, touched Freddy's shoulder, and replied, "A real mur-deroony, boys." Then he looked at Curt, and finally at Ian. "Reckon y'all found me a little speck a' perfection."

Ian could tell just by looking at Freddy and G'Nat's faces that they were busting to tell Ackerman of their Olympia adventure. But, as they had all agreed, they kept their four-cornered secret. As though reading Ian's fearful mind, Ackerman looked at his SOKs and said, "Y'all gotta promise me one thing: Don't ever tell me where y'all got it. They don't grow like this natural." Then he turned to Ian and said, "I'm obliged, son. Mighty obliged. I could lay me down, die tomorrow, and enter Fiddlers Green a happy man."

"Fiddlers what?" G'Nat asked.

"That's jest sailor talk for Paradise," Ackerman replied, as he found his cigarette and began puffing it back to life.

G'Nat sized the delight of the moment, slung his arms around Freddy's shoulders, and began singing, "She takes. . . "

Freddy knew exactly where he was going and joined in ". . . me to Fiddlers Green."

Ackerman pulled a wadded-up measuring tape out of his pants pocket and proceeded to measure the cornerstone.

"Three feet, seven. One foot, five and one-quarter inches, and twelve inches high, exact," he announced as he measured. "Yessir, a little speck of perfection. I'm obliged."

Ian didn't think Ackerman had been obliged to very many people in his life, but his words were sincere and his green eyes were reflecting an honest gratitude.

"It's only a friggin' rock," Ian said, shifting his glance toward the cove.

"Time will tell, time will tell," Ackerman said. This time the corners of his mouth edged up ever so slightly.

"So *now* can we get started on it?" Freddy asked with an impatient sigh.

"First thing in the mornin'," Ackerman replied. "Come on, Kamicurzi, let's you an' me go study on it. Reckon you boys earned yerselfs a good long swim."

The younger boys issued "finally" and "about time," and followed Ackerman, leaving Ian and Curt to exchange triumphant glances over the cornerstone, the greatest coup of their young careers.

twenty

The next morning, the five from Deerslayer went to the storage shed and started to pull out supplies for building the monolithic structure. The Roswell board of directors, delighted to be free of the fireplace task, had graciously provided the necessary items: an old, rusty mortar box, square shovels, wheel barrels, trowels, a spirit level, a mason's line and pins, and a magnificent wooden block and tackle with new, strong rope for hoisting the rock. Ackerman looked at the line and pins with a vague curiosity.

"Now what'd y'all reckon these is for?" he asked the boys, holding one of the sharp brass pins up and watching it swing on the heavy line.

He passed it around, and each boy's guess was more ludicrous than the previous. "It's something to keep something level, somehow," Curt finally concluded vaguely.

"That's cheatin'. Toss 'er out," Ackerman replied.

With the mortar-building supplies laid out on the grass next to the rock pile, Ackerman, the general addressing his troops, said, "Men, I been studyin' on this. Curt, you an' Eeeon start smoothing down fer the cornerstone right there where I marked out, an' Freddy an' G'Nat start stirring up that ceement."

"Well, I see you're ready to begin!" Hyatt interrupted as he clipped around the corner of the lodge and
saw the SOKs. He stood with his hands on his hips,
reminding Ian of Teddy Roosevelt in his bully, grinning
enthusiasm. Kamicurzi the Kurious approached Hyatt
with a friendly offer of play. Hyatt tried to shoo the
animal away and said to Ackerman, "I thought I asked
you to get rid of that dog."

"Keeps wanderin' on back, Harry," Ackerman said,
not even looking at Hyatt. Ian could tell by the tone in
Ackerman's voice, he wasn't any more fond of Hyatt
than he was.

"Well, Andy, you know the rules," Hyatt concluded,
and then focused again on the project. "So, I see you're
setting up. Now, I thought. . . "

"Now jest who's milkin' this cow, Harry," Ackerman
said, abruptly cutting him off. "This here's our chimney.
Let us alone."

Ian and Curt stopped their work to watch the
adults.

But, as Ian expected, Hyatt was quick to back down.
"Of course, of course. But the board was wondering. . . "

"Now lemme lay out this racket to ya, Harry, so's
ya cain't say I never tol' ya. This here project'll be jest
fine an' dandy, providin' you and yer board keep yer
damn noses outa it."

Ian watched Ackerman continue to set out the
masonry tools. Hyatt came a little closer, as though seeing his shadow on the ground might make Ackerman
look up at him while he spoke. "Well, frankly, Andy, I
got a little concerned when I found the blueprint all
crumpled up in the kitchen trash can."

G'Nat swonked Freddy on the arm, but Ackerman, now making freehand sketches on a clipboard, simply replied coolly, "Now, Harry, why don't you jest run along an' leave us men to our work?"

Hyatt, ruffling a bit now, came a step closer to Ackerman, not to show force, but so he could speak without the SOKs hearing. Ian stepped closer, too.

"Andy," Hyatt began, "how can those boys learn to respect their superiors when you show nothing but contempt for yours?"

He didn't wait for an answer, for, no doubt, he knew what it would be. Ackerman looked at Ian, squinting an eye against his cigarette smoke, or perhaps it was a wink, and said, "Gotta *find* a superior first." Then, to the other three stirring cement, "How's that ceement comin' over there?"

"How'll we know when it's ready?" G'Nat asked, stirring the thick mass with a paddle nearly as large as him.

"Is it hard set yet?"

"No," Freddy answered.

"Then it's ready. But we gotta work fast."

He went to the base to inspect Ian and Curt's work. He knelt, smoothed the sandy surface with his hand as though to judge levelness or, for all Ian knew, warmth and the dirt's ability to hold the cornerstone in its embrace. Kamicurzi looked at the surface and tried to elicit play.

"Dang it. Stop it, dog!" Ackerman sat back and threw a rock for him. Then, looking up at the boys, he said, "Reckon it's time. Eeeon. Y'all back the truck on down here close as ya can."

Ian moved the truck and took the tarp off the cornerstone. It seemed to have grown in magnificence overnight. Standing alone in the truck bed, Ian knelt by the stone and ran his hand down its surface as he'd seen Ackerman do the day before. "Hope you have enough courage," he whispered to it. Then, feeling a rush of stupidity for talking to a rock, he called the others over for assistance.

All five were needed to ease the stone out of the truck. It crashed with a heavy thump as it hit the soft ground, then rolled easily, end over end, downhill until it came to a stop not far from its final resting place.

"Lookit there. She knows where she belongs," Ackerman said in a whisper of amazement. Freddy and G'Nat looked at each other, then cast their eyes identically toward the heavens. Curt circled his ear with his index finger. But Ian could neither laugh, nor ridicule, nor disagree.

Ackerman looked down at the cornerstone's beauty. The sun reflected a myriad tiny dark sparkles off the well-chiseled surface, as though the day it was created black diamonds rained from the sky.

It took straining and groaning and an honest amount of swearing, but the huge cornerstone was quickly set into place. As the base of the structure would be on a slight incline, the cornerstone was laid at the lowest point, its flatness, its strength, its courage thereby supporting the bulk of the weight to come.

The fun part, as the boys had anticipated, was the placing of the rocks and the sloshing around in the cool mortar. Somewhat like working a giant, three-dimensional jigsaw puzzle, each rock was hand-picked to order and placed in a sticky, generous bed of mortar. Ackerman would occasionally stand back and eye-assess the levelness of each layer as the foundation took shape and grew higher and higher.

With the chimney growing at the approximate rate of three feet a day, it finally became necessary to implement a hoist. Hyatt had provided them with the old flagpole which, once secured to the roof of the lodge and anchored to the ground, held the block and tackle. Swinging from the rope was a wooden box which held the rocks and buckets of mortar as they were hoisted up.

Ian and G'Nat worked at the top of the structure, while Curt and Freddy worked below, mixing, choosing the rocks, and pulling them up. Kamikurzi stood around, a rock always in his mouth, hoping someone would take notice of him and feel obliged to throw it.

When the chimney got too high to climb, the boys too were hoisted up: Ian, by hanging onto the rope like Tarzan, followed by G'Nat using the box as a boatswain's chair.

Ackerman worked on the firebox inside the lodge, building an intricate, herring-bone pattern out of fire-bricks. Hyatt had brought down the radio from the Admin Hall and, although the reception was fuzzy, they were able to get some music and war news, finally, from a Seattle station.

Every now and then a tune, especially a ballad, would catch Ackerman's ear and he would hum along absently as he worked. From the other side of the structure, Ian could hear his smooth voice, sometimes clear, sometimes slurred, and wondered how he had come to know so many songs. It astonished him that Ackerman's southern drawl was so thick that he even hummed with an accent. When no music could be coaxed from the radio dial, Ackerman would begin his inevitable "Paradise," and the boys would dutifully da-daa after each line of Ackerman's theme song.

Once the rockery had reached the top of the firebox, the construction became more exact and difficult. They began creating the chimney itself. The higher it became, the narrower it became, until finally the work had to be done from scaffolding. At this point, Ian and Curt took turns laying the rocks while Freddy, who had become a master of mortar, took charge of the mixing.

G'Nat, who had taken such care in choosing the smaller, rounder rocks from the beach and the smooth, glossy stones from the stream beds, was in charge of constructing the rockery around the firebox. The mantel shelf was a sanded log, cut in half, smelling of forest and offering a fine ledge for decoration.

As the days passed, Ian kept a closer eye on Ackerman. He got so he could tell when Ackerman was merely blurry because of his pain pills and when he was out-and-out loaded on morphine. He could tell by his eyes, those green daggers that he had first glared into — full of rage, full of challenge, and now full of desperate last will. If the others noticed anything, Ian was quick to remind them of Wackerman's screwy behavior.

* * *

Seventeen days from the laying of the cornerstone, the Deerslayers had deep tans, new muscles, calloused hands, injured fingers, sailors' vocabularies, and an unparalleled sense of accomplishment in themselves as a team and as individuals.

They had been blessed with warm weather, which had allowed the giant structure to grow, dry, and cure without interruption. Although there had been a few days of Puget Sound morning drizzle, it hadn't hampered the project and, if ever a summer had been perfect for such an undertaking, Hyatt gushed, it had been that summer.

The difficult part was waiting for a week to pass for the structure to thoroughly set and dry before the inaugural fire could be set. Even the campers who had shown little enthusiasm for the project were growing restless for the chosen night.

The SOKs hardly ever showed up at the campfire ritual, the evensong. Even though, by dusk, they had long since put away their rockery tools, they took full advantage of their non-camper carte blanche and stayed away from institutional activities. They'd swim or boat under Ackerman's casual supervision, or hike around camp, set their own records on the obstacle course, or hang out in Deerslayer, relaxing from their days of backbreaking work, drinking beer, passing around dime novels, and discussing women, war, and the wages of sin.

But with the project now finished, and out of the boredom that familiarity and close quarters bring, the four SOKs decided to join in the campfire a few nights before the fireplace was to be inaugurated.

G'Nat and Freddy were given a worshiping hero's welcome by some of the younger campers, and they melted easily into the rows of boys seated around the giant campfire. Both Ian and Curt instinctively held back, content to watch the evening's activities from the shadows of the surrounding forest.

Ackerman, Ian noticed, was nowhere in the circle of firelight.

Hyatt made a few compulsory announcements, cracked some tired, tame camp jokes, and led the now boring, perfected songs. A man in his element, Ian thought.

He nudged Curt at his side and asked, "What do you suppose this guy does when camp is over?"

Curt stared at Hyatt, gave the question some serious consideration, then finally answered, "Hibernates."

It was the only logical answer, and Ian broke out in hearty laughter. Since the song the campers were singing was a quiet little hymn, Ian and Curt immediately retreated further back into the woods, and tried to stifle their laughter.

The hymn was followed by 'impromptu' skits which each cabin-load of boys had, no doubt, worked on all day. No prize for the best, just applause from the rest of the campers and Hyatt's resounding accolades. G'Nat and Freddy were quickly asked to join the boys of another cabin. They huddled together, giggling and planning their skits.

"We have more talent scratching fleas on the floor of Deerslayer than all those other cabins put together," Curt said.

Ian looked quizzically at Curt. "The mutt?" he asked incredibly.

"Yeah. Not to mention any of us."

"Well, don't get any ideas about *us* getting up and doing some stupid skit," Ian warned. "I'm not making a fool of myself in front of this or any other crowd."

Ian walked in closer and, pointing to Freddy and G'Nat, said, "Lookit those twerps. Fine SOKs they turned out to be."

Curt laughed at their antics on stage and replied, "Yeah. A coupla' naturals. The next Abbott and Costello. Freddy's a born ad-libber."

"Come on, Curt, all this makes me puke. Let's go for a swim," Ian coaxed. "Water's warm as piss on a night like this."

"Waterfront's closed. Shsss. Watch this."

"Bet I can beat you on the obstacle course. . . "

"Off limits at night, you know that."

Ian, feeling Curt's defection all but upon him, pulled his arm, and said, "Rules, rules, rules. . . "

"No, I want to lob around here for awhile. Go on ahead. Take a swim. I'll keep Hyatt outa your hair."

Ian looked at Curt, then at the siren song of the snapping, blazing campfire. Curt stepped into the circle of light, and his appearance was cheered by the others.

Ian slipped deeper into the darkness. He let his eyes adjust to the shadows before picking his way down the path toward Deerslayer, wondering why he was so repelled by the campfire, the camaraderie of those around it, and the boyish times the campers were sharing. It was almost as if having the giant fireplace to build was the only way he could tolerate being at Roswell. As though

their quest, their mission made good, tolerable sense . . .
a reason to be there. Better yet, a reason not to be anywhere else. But now, with the project completed, 'none
a' this camp shit for me,' he thought, hearing Ackerman's
accent.

Ian turned his thoughts to Ackerman. It had been
the same with him. He knew it had. He was more sullen
and withdrawn since the last rock had been carefully laid.
He disappeared more often and stayed away longer. His
magnificent eyes had now totally lost their zealous,
contagious fire, and Ian noticed how his hands shook
constantly now as he lit one cigarette off the butt of
another.

The mornings were cooler. August was nearly over.
Camp was coming to an end. And Ackerman was dying.

twenty-one

It came as no surprise to Ian after his escape from the campfire that he ended up in the darkened lodge. He wanted to have the chimney, the fireplace, the memories to himself. The large room was cool, clean, and dimly lit. The tables had been pushed alongside the walls so that the floors could be mopped, and the light came from a small lamp sitting on the piano, also now pushed back against the wall next to the fireplace.

Ian stole a bottle of milk from the cooler, pulled a large chair over from a corner, and sat, legs outstretched, staring into the empty, chaste fireplace. The sounds of camp harmony came drifting in through the open windows . . . how many times had Ian heard that same campfire song? Fifty? A hundred? A million times?

". . . I was born about ten thousand years ago . . . there ain't a thing in this world that I don't know . . . I saw Peter, Paul, and Moses playing ring-a-round the roses . . . And I can whip the guy that says it isn't so . . . "

A smile started to crawl over his face, for, from the safe distance, maybe the words were, well, maybe just a little funny . . . but the rhythm, the tune, the smile faded with the words from the darkest corner of the room, "I jest reckon you ain't the campfire type, Eeeon."

Ian kept looking into the blankness of the fireplace and replied, "Reckon you ain't either, Andy."

Ackerman walked toward him. Kamicurzi clicked along at his side in dare-me defiance to Hyatt's precious camp rules. Ackerman stopped at the piano and spread his fingers a generous octave-and-a-half across the keys. He keyed a few bars of "Paradise," then sat down against the rockery of the fireplace. He pulled out his pack of Camels and his silver-and-turquoise lighter, lit up, and slid them both over to Ian.

"Smoke?"

Ian looked at the cigarettes, took one, lit it, stifled a cough, and tried to exhale a smoke ring.

Ackerman, seeing the lopsided affair, said, "Nope, ya gotta let yer tongue do the work, boy. . . " And he blew a set of six perfectly round rings of smoke.

Ian tried again, didn't do much better, and Ackerman said, "I'd hate to think all ya learnt at camp was how to blow them damn rings a' smoke."

Ian looked beyond Ackerman and replied, "I learned how to build a fireplace. That skill ought to get me real far in the war."

"War'll be over before yer old enough to join up."

"There'll be other wars and I'll be in them."

Ian kept staring into the fireplace, and he knew Ackerman was staring at him in the silence.

Then Ackerman said, "I believe you will, son. So, what branch you plannin' on honorin' with yer presence?"

"Navy," Ian replied, a little faster than he'd wished. Then, jokingly, he added, "Hey, did I ever tell you my dad's in the Navy? Commodore McKenzie. Maybe you've heard of him. I hear he's saving our ass in the Philippines."

"Do tell."

"Yep. So I'll be going to Annapolis. You know, family tradition and all."

"Yer camp file says yer a pretty smart son of a bitch. Maybe Annapolis ain't so much a joke," Ackerman said, his voice scrabbly now and serious.

Ian looked at him, slid the cigarettes and lighter back at him with a snap of his wrist, and said, "I couldn't get appointed to throw that dog in the pound, let alone Annapolis, Ackerman."

"Ya never know. . . "

"Yes I do. Look, I don't think you read the rest of my camp file, Ackerman. My dad was a grease ape, then he took a nice long hike. My mom's a measly waitress, when the fleet's out of town. I'm not exactly officer material, if you know what I mean. Oh yes, one other little problem: I tried to kill a man. Now tell me, if you were a senator, would you appoint me? I'm lucky I didn't get appointed to the state pen."

Ackerman looked long and hard at Ian before he responded, "Yep, I reckon ya are at that."

There came some cheering from the campfire out in the woods. Ian and Ackerman's eyes met and almost smiled. Then Ackerman closed his eyes tight, as a spasm of pain knifed through him.

Ian wasn't as frightened this time and didn't look away. He asked, "Need help, Andy? Bring your morphine?"

Ackerman squeezed his eyes tight, shook his head, and muttered, "Too soon, boy. Gotta get a handle on it."

Even Kamicurzi seemed to know how to handle the spasms now. He simply sat next to his step-master and patiently waited, ears low, eyes searching the room, licking Ackerman's face when the muscles relaxed.

"Ya got evil breath, dog," Ackerman said, smiling and playfully pushing the dog away.

"Okay now?" Ian asked, relieved he wasn't going to have to inject morphine again.

Ackerman smiled and said, "Everythin's copacetic, boy."

Ian waited for a few more moments to pass before he pointed his cigarette toward the fireplace and asked, "What if it doesn't draw smoke?"

Ackerman ran his hands along the still cool surface next to him and answered, "She'll draw. If there's one thing I know, it's smoke." Then, as though to illustrate his point, he dragged hard, held the smoke in his mouth, then slowly let it escape up and into his nose, from which he took it down deep into his lungs.

"That there's a French inhale. Don't know what's so goddam French about it."

Ian took another drag, then aimed his series of smoke rings toward the fireplace. But Ackerman caught them as they leisurely traveled on the draft and said, "No ya don't, Eeeon. She ain't tastin' smoke till she's ready."

"But what if the damn thing doesn't work?" Ian persisted.

"Only one thing ya kin do. Tear her down an' start all over again."

"You can screw that idea, son," Ian said.

"You kin screw a dream, but not a idea," Ackerman drawled. "Nope, if she don't draw, all ya kin do is knock her down an' start all over." He coughed as another brief spasm seized hold of him. "See, it ain't finished till she draws perfect. An' ya gotta have the guts to finish it, Eeeon, even if it means startin' all over with nothin'."

He finally opened his eyes. His face softened some as he looked at Ian. And then he smiled, the first real smile, smile of pleasure, Ian recalled ever seeing on Ackerman's face. "But that ain't gonna happen, son. Jest let her set an' rest a spell till Saturday night an' she'll draw you any fire you place in her lap. Y'all wait an' see."

He rose, steadied himself, and headed for the doors to the deck. He turned, leaned down to pet Kamicurzi, smiled a second time, and repeated, "Y'all wait an' see."

Ian watched the door latch, then dropped his cigarette into the milk bottle. His attention turned back toward the fireplace and he stared into it, again reliving the placement of every rock. Then it occurred to him that they, the Deerslayers, hadn't signed their work. Every work of art, no matter how insignificant, must be signed, he thought.

It took him several hours to etch the names on the rocks with his switchblade. He choose a rock appropriate for each SOK. A beautifully colored agate was 'Curt', a tiny rock holding up two larger ones was 'G'Nat', a perfectly round one was, of course, 'Freddy', and his own, the most difficult one to find, was the blue-gray color of his eyes, deeply set, well hidden, along the wall. So well placed, so careful were his etchings, that surely no one would ever notice. That was fine, he told himself. It wasn't important that even the others knew of his signatures.

He worked late into the night and then fell asleep. When he awoke the next morning to the squawking of some belligerent duck on the waterfront, he found himself stretched out in front of the fireplace, knife in hand and, curiously, a blanket around him.

The deck door opened and Curt came in, ruffled from sleep. He gently kicked Ian's feet and said, "Hey, McKenzie, wake up."

Ian sat up and yawned.

"Ackerman thought you might be here," Curt continued. "What's with you, anyway? Freddy's farting finally drive you out?"

"I must have dozed off," Ian offered, arching his back against the stiffness.

Curt picked up the knife next to Ian and said, "What were you going to do, slit your wrists because camp's almost over?"

"Two more glorious days of this crap," Ian said, pulling his knees to his chest.

"Come on, McKenzie. Why don't you snap out of it and enjoy these last days."

"I am enjoying them. Everything's . . . copacetic."

"Bullshit! You and Ackerman both. What a couple of zombies. Come on, it's Field Day. How's about signing up for the Obstacle Course. I challenge you."

"That's no challenge. G'Nat could beat you with his brace off," Ian replied moodily.

Undaunted, Curt continued. "Well, then there's a shoot off at the Rifle Range. Let's you and me sign up."

Ian got up, stretched, and wandered toward the windows overlooking the cove. He looked out at Hyatt's Chris Craft, and it glimmered back at him seductively.

"Wanna go for a boat ride?" he asked Curt. He looked at him and raised his eyebrows three times, the international signal for 'wanna join me?'

"Oh no you don't. Hyatt'll have our asses," Curt hedged. He stepped back, as though trying to distance himself from even the suggestion of such camp mutiny.

Ian looked at him, shook his head, smiled sadly, and said, "Not one brave thing, Hollenbeck."

He left through the deck doors and walked toward the waterfront.

twenty-two

Curt had called it exactly as it was — Ian and Ackerman both had distanced themselves. After breakfast,
instead of joining in the field day activities or cheering
on their fellow SOKs, they took out a canoe. Ackerman
lay down, his feet up on the seat, his arm crooked across
his eyes to shade them from the sun's bright gaiety. Ian
leisurely paddled them about, in and out of the cove's
scalloped edges, hearing now and then cheers from the
warring groups above.

Ackerman's body suddenly stiffened and Ian whirled
around to see him rigid with pain, in the midst of a
seizure. The spells were coming on quicker and more
violent.

"Ackerman, you okay?"

Ackerman gained control, pulled out his hypo box,
and prepared an injection.

"You just did that two hours ago," Ian said, placing
the paddle across his lap. "Why can't I get you back to
Madigan? They gotta have something. . ." He stopped
talking and watched as Ackerman injected the morphine.

Ian felt his eyes tear. He clenched his jaw and
looked away.

Ackerman relaxed, leaned his hand over the canoe,

splashed some water on his face, and then swished some up at Ian.

Startled by the cold water, Ian said, "Hey! Knock it off!"

Ackerman was smiling at him. "I'd hate to think a' you loosin' yer sensa humor, Eeeon. Why don't you jest let me worry about this," he added, holding up the black case, "an' you jest worry 'bout bein' a kid?"

His candid words stunned Ian. It was as though as long as Ian didn't talk about it, Ackerman's mortal wound would simply disappear. It didn't make any sense — such a small speck of metal. He couldn't even see the scar from the original wound on his head. It was hard for Ian to believe that anyone could die from what amounted to only a little more than a sliver. Slivers are supposed to fester, then simply pop out.

Ian didn't reply, but returned to his paddling.

"Try not to hit them ruts in the road," Ackerman added. This time a broad grin.

Ian laughed and replied, "We'll go over there. They just paved it."

Then, his voice shaky now, Ackerman continued, "The pisser a' this is, one minute I'm okay, the next my head's rippin' apart."

They were interrupted by Freddy's shrill voice from across the cove: "Hey, you guys!"

"'Course, that voice'd give anyone a headache," Ackerman said.

Freddy stood on the dock, chubby hands cupped to sunburned cheeks. He had three shiny ribbons pinned to his chest, signifying participation in something or the other, and standing next to him was a panting Kamicurzi.

Ian paddled closer and called back, "What d'you want?"

"Curt's made it to the finals at the Rifle Range! Will you guys take this stupid dog for me? He's being a real pain in the ass." He held up the dog's leash. "The goddam stupid dog keeps trying to snap at the rifle muzzles! Curt can't concentrate with all his yapping!"

Ian looked at Ackerman, who replied, "Let's go in, Eeeon. Don't wanna git too sunburned out here. 'Sides, Curt needs hisself a ribbon. I got me some things to do, anyhow."

"You guys coming up to watch or not?" Freddy demanded.

Ian docked the canoe, and Ackerman jumped out as cavalierly as though he was about to embark on a seven-day's leave in an Oriental port. Then he swayed, as though to regain his balance; he put his hand to his head, and the sailor's leave was over.

"I'll be up by 'n' by, son," Ackerman said kindly to Freddy. "I see ya got yerself a fine looking fruit salad, there." He lifted a few of the ribbons and added, "Ian'll be happy to watch Kamicurzi. I got me errands to run."

"Happy?" Ian asked, watching Ackerman disappear.

Freddy tossed the leash toward him and took off up hill toward the Rifle Range. "I gotta blow, Ian. G'Nat and me're Curt's gunloaders. Keep that damn dog away, okay? He's driving us all nutty and Hyatt's wandering all around."

Ian tied off the dog, pulled the canoe in, and watched Ackerman walk along the waterfront toward the Admin Hall. His stride wasn't young and arrogant like it should have been; it was rickety and unsure, an old man's shuffle.

Where to now? It wasn't going to be the Rifle Range — Curt didn't need him around to win anything. It wasn't going to be baseball, leathercrafts, rowboat races, nor was it going to be reading, thoughtful retrospection of another summer gone by, growth, war, school.

It was going to be the chimney and the final task: carving Ackerman's name on his stone, the only stone, the cornerstone. He lay in the cool dirt, still footprinted and muddy from the construction, and worked with his knife, dulled now from the previous night's work. But he stayed on task, and halfway through wondered if maybe he shouldn't have just carved 'Andy' instead of the lengthier 'Ackerman.'

Laying next to him, under protest, was Kamicurzi, who with every ring from the Rifle Range would bark wildly, begging for freedom. No amount of rock throwing, verbal or physical chastising, could silence the dog. Finally, Ian simply ignored the dog and finished his work.

"Whatcha'all doin' down there, son?" Ackerman asked, startling Ian.

Ian sat up and hid his knife. "Just seeing if she's settled any, that's all. What's in the box?"

"Beer, peanuts, ice," Ackerman replied, looking into the wood box he was carrying. "Party fixin's. Here, take it on up to Deerslayer. Whatever ya do, don't let ol' man Hyatt see ya with that stuff. Or else."

Ian looked at the beer bottles poking up and said, "Curt's gonna love you."

As Ian walked up toward Deerslayer, watching out for Hyatt and the counselors, he noticed a calm, a pall almost, had come over the camp. The shooting had stopped, and no more sudden rises of faraway cheers could be heard. Since the afternoon was drawing to a close, no doubt the winners had all been declared.

When he reached Deerslayer, he saw Freddy and G'Nat sitting on the steps. He knew by their posture that something was wrong. His first and only assumption was, they had found out about Ackerman.

He approached them cautiously and asked, "Hey, what's up?

"Nice job of hanging onto Kamicurzi, McKenzie!" Freddy hollered down at him.

Ian thought about the dog, shrugged his shoulders, and said coolly, defensively, "Oh yeah, guess he took off. He wasn't happy with me anyhow. . . " He started to walk up the steps and slowed when he saw the tears streaming down G'Nat's tiny face.

"I don't think you better go in there," he said with the sniff of one who's trying his damnedest not to cry.

"Why? What's wrong?"

"Kamicurzi, you jerk. . . " G'Nat said.

"So what the hell happened?" Ian demanded.

"Curt shot him!" G'Nat cried back.

Freddy, also fighting tears said, "You let him go, Ian! I *told* you that stupid dog was snapping at the guns! You let him go and now he's dead!"

"I thought you were bullshitting about that snapping at guns!"

Freddy looked up at him and said solemnly, "I wasn't lying, Ian!"

Of all the horrors that had crossed Ian's troubled mind that day, losing the dog, the foundling, their fellow SOK, wasn't one of them.

He took another step and G'Nat, crying openly now, said, "It was awful . . . he wasn't dead at first, Ian! So Curt had to shoot him again!" He ran his sleeve over his face and added, "He had to kill him."

Freddy looked out over the hillside, threw a pine cone he'd been fidgeting with, and said, "You *know* how much Andy loved that dog! He's going to die when he finds out!"

G'Nat picked up the collar and leash he'd woven in leathercrafts, threw them forcefully against the cabin, and said, "Ain't no use for these!"

When Ian continued up the steps, Freddy warned him, "You're the *last* person he wants to see, McKenzie!"

"Look, get lost, you guys!" Ian ordered.

"We don't have to!" Freddy screamed back. Ian started for him with a raised fist and they both took off down the steps.

G'Nat picked up a rock and threw it at Ian. "You fucking son of a bitch!" he screamed for all he was worth. Then, with Freddy helping him along, he limped off into the woods.

Ian turned and slowly pushed the door open with his foot. Inside, Curt was lying on his bunk, staring at the ceiling.

"Get the fuck out of here."

Ian placed the box on Ackerman's bunk and popped one of the quarts of beer. He held it up and offered it to Curt.

"Beer, Hollenbeck? It's cold."

Curt placed his arm over his eyes and quietly began to shake. "Get lost."

Ian saw a tear fall down the side of his face and knew, were the situation reversed, he'd want to be alone. He started to leave, then said, "Look, Curt, I'm sorry, all right? I'm sorry." He tried to put as much sincerity into his voice as he could, but he was more concerned about how Ackerman would react.

"You never liked that dog," Curt said, his jaw flexing as he struggled to hold his grief and anger inside.

"He just snuck away, that's all. You know that dog could slip a hitch if he wanted to. I just didn't notice, that's all. I'm sorry. Besides. . . "

"There ain't no 'besides,' McKenzie," Curt replied, his voice whispering now.

"No, I guess there ain't," he said, looking out the window toward the waterfront. He noticed a gold medal dangling from Curt's bunk. He picked it up and said, "I see you did it."

"Did what?"

"Took first."

Curt didn't respond, but rather rolled toward the window and, running his finger along the sash, said, "He was Ackerman's dog anyway. . . "

Ian put the medal down, opened the door, and said, "Yeah." He quietly closed the door behind him and took the path down.

He had other confessions, other amends, yet to make that day.

twenty-three

By the time Ian found Ackerman, Hyatt had already informed him of the stray's unfortunate demise.

Ian saw him walking uphill toward Deerslayer. Ackerman stopped in the path and let Ian speak. "I'm sorry, Ackerman! I guess he just took off. I didn't even see him go. I'm sorry." Ian held his ground and illustrated his point with his arms.

All Ackerman said was a cool, morphined, "Leave it go, boy." He walked past Ian, and Ian, his rage building, whirled him back around by the arm.

"I can't just leave it go, damn it! I thought Freddy was lying about that gun snapping. . . "

But Ackerman's eyes were red and fiery and almost vague in their focus. He touched Ian's hand upon his arm and said again, "I said, leave it go, son."

He kept walking uphill, and Ian called out after him, tears in his own eyes now, "But I'm sorry, Andy!"

Alone now in the chill of the sunless woods, Ian's eyes came to rest on the sign that pointed uphill and cheerfully announced 'Rifle Range.' He lunged for the sign, ripped it off, smashed it in half against a tree, and heaved the pieces into the brush.

What angered him, confused him, was that Ackerman, kneeling now in the dawn of his own death, was so affected by the death of Kamicurzi . . . a dog, a stray, a three-legged mutt.

Not surprisingly, Curt didn't go down to dinner that evening. Ackerman chose to stay with him on the porch of Deerslayer. Although Ian had no appetite at all, he knew he had to be a presence in the dining hall that evening, in the absence of Andy and Curt, in case Hyatt dared to sermonize the day's loss — which is exactly what he did.

After dinner, Ian asked the cook for two trays to take up to Deerslayer, should Curt and Ackerman get hungry later, and since there was only one more dinner to prepare that summer, the trays were laden with odds and ends.

Ian sent Freddy and G'Nat back up to the cabin with the food and, unsure what to do next, decided to follow, but lag behind and out of sight.

Ackerman and Curt were sitting on the porch of Deerslayer when Freddy and G'Nat arrived with the trays. There were two beer bottles on the porch between them.

"Hope you guys are hungry. These weigh a ton," G'Nat said, setting down a tray on the steps.

"Might have myself a bite," Ackerman said.

Ian, still hidden on the trail below, could tell just by looking at his eyes, listening to his slick drawl, that Ackerman was still loaded with morphine. He wondered if he'd told Curt.

Then Ian heard little G'Nat's voice pipe up, now praising, now adoring, not cursing, not damning. "You should have heard Ian at dinner, Curt! When ol' man Hyatt starting yapping about why dogs ain't allowed at camp. . . "

"On accounta they can get hurt," Freddy jumped in.

"Freddy, let *me* tell it! How he'd warned and warned and warned us about that stray mutt. Anyway, ol' Ian just stands right up and interrupts Hyatt. Said that he thought he was missing the whole point. Said if he ever got off his goddam box fulla camp bullshit, he'd understand."

"He said horse shit," Freddy corrected.

"Shut up! Some kinda shit! Anyway, Ian takes off on him like he's Churchill and ol' man Hyatt's Mussolini — a goddam dictator, he calls him."

"Tell 'em the part about being brave," Freddy urged, pulling out a chicken leg and relishing it as much as G'Nat's version of the story.

"Oh yeah. Ian says Curt's *forgotten* more about bravery than Hyatt'll ever even know! Said putting a dog down like that takes guts, plain an' simple. Guts!"

G'Nat and Freddy waited for that to sink in before Freddy added the coup de grace: "The whole damn room went wild! Every boy cheered and hollered and clapped! It was mur-der!"

"Yeah," G'Nat summed up, "they cheered Curt for having the guts and Ian for shutting ol' man Hyatt up once and for all. It was really slick."

Ian walked out from the forest shadows, and Curt, upon seeing him, stared coldly down. Then, slowly, a smile came across his face. Ackerman watched Curt and Ian watched Ackerman.

Curt stood up, held out a beer, and asked, "Beer, McKenzie? It's still cold."

"Yeah, thanks," he said, and in so saying was welcomed back into the arms of Deerslayer and back into Ackerman's and Curt's graces.

After a few rounds of beer, Ackerman finally slurred down to Ian, "Yer bein' mighty quiet down there, Eeeon."

"Sssh," Ian said. "Holy shit! Hyatt's coming!"

"Christ, stow them dead soldiers," Ackerman ordered.

They scrambled to ditch the beer bottles, and Ian dove into the cabin to slam close and lock his footlocker, which held other contraband.

Puffing somewhat from the climb, Hyatt greeted the Deerslayers just as Ian eased back out onto the porch.

Hyatt gave him a chilly look, but spoke to Ackerman and the other Deerslayers. "I see everyone's present and accounted for. Just dropped by to see if everything is . . . a . . . all right up here," he said.

No one replied, so Hyatt continued, his face falling back into its natural frown, "Now, Curt, I wanted to tell you I'm sorry I reacted the way I did over that dog. I've been asking you Deerslayers to get rid of it all along. Just so something like this didn't have to happen." He looked at the SOKs, then added, softer, less official, "Son, nobody comes out to camp to see a dog get shot."

"Well, I didn't exactly come out here to shoot one, either," Curt replied, not as forcefully as Ian thought he would have.

"Of course you didn't. You see, son, lots of the boys here this summer won't have the opportunity of coming back next year. They'll be knee-deep in the war. Some of them might even be dead . . . killed in action. You can understand how my only job here is that they have the time of their lives. Death is the last thing I want my boys to see. And, I suppose, that's why I lost my head and said those things up at the Rifle Range." He paused and attempted a smile. "Well, I just didn't want you going home without hearing my side."

Ian couldn't believe Curt was going to let Hyatt leave without accepting his apology or, at least, should he possibly be too drunk to speak coherently, give him a nod. Instead, Curt just stared blankly at the man.

"Oh, by the way, while I have you boys all here," Hyatt continued, his face brighter, "everything is all set for tomorrow night. The big ceremony for the fireplace. Now, it's your party, so don't dawdle." He looked directly at Curt and added, "It would be nice if you were all there to share the honors."

He said good night and turned to leave.

"Mr. Hyatt?" Curt called out. Hyatt stopped and turned. "I'm sorry I called you a mother fuc. . . " he caught himself, then continued, "what I called you."

Hyatt visibly cringed, but said calmly, "Please, don't mention it."

After he was well out of earshot, Ian turned to Curt and asked with an incredulous grin, "You called him that? Now *that* was brave!"

"Now, it's *you* might be missin' the point, son," Ackerman said, slipping another pill into his mouth without being seen by the others.

There was silence as their eyes were drawn to the pink sunset to the west.

Finally, Ackerman rose and asked, "Who all wants a beer?"

"Me!" Freddy and G'Nat chorused, hands held high.

"I got y'all some fizz. Come on in an' pick it out. You know, Freddy, I think this here creme soda tastes sorta like marshmellers." He escorted the younger ones inside.

Curt and Ian's eyes fell on one another and there was an awkward air between them. They each took a quart of beer and, leaving the youngers to Ackerman, wandered down to the waterfront.

They sat on one of the overturned rowboats on the shore and threw rocks at the flecks of moonlight on the water.

"What I would like to have done was give him a Viking burial," Curt finally said, one-hundred-and-eighty degrees away from their discussion of rock-skipping.

"So where'd you bury him?" Ian asked.

"Up by the baseball diamond," Curt answered, head down, voice low.

"I should go up and pay my respects," Ian replied somberly.

"You'd never find the grave."

"You marked it, didn't you?" He leaned over and looked at Curt.

"What'd you want me to do, carve a goddam cross?" Curt snapped sarcastically. He'd consumed far more than his share of beer that evening.

"Well, we have a lot of good rocks left over," Ian baited.

"So?"

"So we can't just leave Kamicurzi in an unmarked

grave, for God's sake! He's a goddam hero! He practically died in the line of duty!" Ian said, standing up and brushing the sand off his pants.

"Correction," Curt slurred: "he died in the line of the *bullet's* duty."

Ian looked at him and challenged once more, perhaps for the last time, "You with me or not?"

Curt looked up the hill toward Deerslayer, dark now and asleep. "What about the twerps?"

"We'll haul their butts out of bed to help. No mortar like Freddy mortar."

"And Ackerman?"

Ian remembered how drugged he'd appeared earlier and wondered if he'd even be able to pull him awake. "Wall," he drawled, "he's either with us or agin us."

He was with them.

When they were sure that all the adults had turned in, Curt and Ian woke their fellow SOKs. Freddy mixed a wheelbarrow full of mortar while the other boys quietly chose a quantity of rocks to haul up to the baseball diamond. They swiped as many lanterns as they could find around the shed and, quickly and quietly, they set off. Going silently single-file through the woods with their loads and swinging lanterns, they cast strange shadows through the camp, looking much like the restless ghosts of lost gold miners.

Once Curt had located the grave, they set about their task. Ackerman sat off in the distance, watching his men work. He smoked and said nothing.

Quietly, professionally, with a seasoned sense of commitment, they covered the grave with a layer of flat stones, followed by a layer of the smaller, oval ones that

G'Nat had specialized in. Before long and with only minimal talk, the gravestone, a small replica of the chimney, had been erected.

They placed lanterns all around the grave to highlight its genius. Ackerman stood at the head and Curt at the foot. Ackerman passed the last bottle of beer around, now allowing the younger ones to partake of the sacred brew.

"I just want to say," Ian began, "that here lies one hell of a dog." He took a gulp of beer and passed the bottle to Curt.

Curt drank and then said, "A courageous dog." He passed the bottle to G'Nat.

"A three-legged dog," he said, handing the bottle across to Freddy.

But Freddy griped, "Say something nice, you dope!"

"But he *was* a three-legged dog. Hell, that's two more'n me." He snatched back the bottle, took another slug, and repeated, "Here's to a three-legged dog!"

Freddy took back the bottle, drank, and said, "Okay, here's to a . . . truthful dog." He passed the bottle back to Ackerman.

Ackerman held the bottle up high in praise and said, "I been studyin' on it. Kamicurzi worked all day on catchin' him that bullet. So, here lies a successful dog. May we all die knowin' success."

From his reverent, downward glance, Ian looked over at Ackerman.

Ackerman was looking right at him. In the lantern light, his face was warm and alive and young. He smiled at Ian and winked.

After the service, the boys scrambled to clean up

their gear. The pre-dawn birds were already beginning to make their bids to claim the day, and there was the faint pinkness of a sailor-take-warning sunrise.

Ackerman was the last to leave the grave, sweeping away some stray pebbles. Ian looked back and asked, "Hey, you coming?"

He waved Ian off and said, "You head on down. I'll be there by an' by."

Ian turned, oddly vindicated. Then, as an after-thought, he turned back and saw Ackerman, kneeling now, his head cradled in his arms, weeping openly over the grave of Kamicurzi.

twenty-four

Hyatt had a full last day planned for the Roswell camp-ers. Boys hustled from relays to races, waterfront to crafts, tennis to archery. Followed by time spent cleaning out cabins and footlockers, packing, and resting for the barbecue and First Fire ceremony ahead.

G'Nat and Freddy huddled on their bunks and made plans to continue their friendship in Tacoma where, since G'Nat was a foster-home kid, maybe Freddy's parents would adopt him, and the team could go on forever.

Ian smiled on their simple solution to the problems of their lives in the city and silently wished them well. He and Curt made plans, exchanged phone numbers, and vowed to hold their friendship above the crosstown rivalry of their schools.

"What do you suppose Ackerman will do now that summer's over?" Curt asked.

He hadn't told him, after all, Ian thought. Good. Good. "Oh, he said he was going to catch up with his ship in the Pacific." It was an easy lie.

"Lucky son of a gun," Curt said, sorting through his footlocker. He tossed Ian a few peanuts he had found and said, "Guess we'll never know what happened to him in the war."

"Guess not," Ian said, folding a towel, aching with the pain of Ackerman's secret.

"Where's he been today, anyway?" Curt asked.

"He told me he'd be over at the lodge, helping Hyatt set up for tonight. He said he wouldn't trust anybody but himself to lay that fire."

"What if it doesn't draw?" Freddy asked, his chubby face wrinkled with concern. "What if we're all sitting there and we light the fire and the whole lodge fills up with smoke?"

"What if the fire blows right into the lodge and we're all burnt to a crisp?" G'Nat joined in, grasping his throat and falling over dead on his bunk.

Ian tossed his pillow at the pessimists and said, "Then we all tear her down, stone by stone, and rebuild her."

Curt reached into the corner of Freddy's footlocker and pulled out some stray marshmallows so old they were good projectiles, and he added, tossing them at the younger boys, "And we're going to use these for the foundation!"

The cooks had planned a wonderful outdoor meal. A local farmer had donated a side of beef that had to be turned on a spit, each boy taking a scorching turn at the handle. Corn on the cob from local fields, clams from the beach below, freshly baked bread, and watermelon filled out the menu. As the sun began to fade into the forest across the cove, the boys began to draw into a closer circle around the huge bonfire just outside the lodge.

Eventually, the camp songs began, and as they did Ian backed out of the circle.

"Now, boys, may I have your attention?" Hyatt finally broke in. "As you know, this, our last night here at Camp Roswell, is a doubly special occasion. I know we're all enjoying this campfire, but we're going to put it out now and adjourn to the lodge for our celebration. The more of you help with clean-up duty, the sooner we can begin. And, I might add, cook has been busy all day with a special cake."

Ian wandered back to Deerslayer to tell Ackerman it was time. He called his name out and pushed open the door, but he wasn't there. Ian felt his heart jerk inside him when he saw an envelope peeking out from under his pillow. He knew. He knew without reading it that Ackerman had left. With trembling hands, he picked it up.

"Hey, McKenzie!" Curt called out from the bottom of the hill. "You coming or what?"

Ian, startled, called back from the porch. "Yeah yeah!"

"Where's Ackerman?" Curt bellowed.

Ian stuffed the envelope into his shirt and ran down the path to Curt. "Ah . . . he said he'll catch up. Start without him." The most difficult lie of his life.

"What a screwball," said Curt, shaking his head. Then he turned and eagerly led the way to the lodge.

But Ian couldn't follow yet. He had to read the letter.

"Come on, Ian!" Curt called when he noticed that his friend wasn't behind him.

"Look, I gotta take a leak. I'll be there. Go ahead."

"All right, but Hyatt said they can't start until we're *all* there." And he ran on back to the lodge.

When Ian walked into the gaiety of the lodge a few minutes later, he was nearly bowled over with cheers and adulations. They had indeed been impatiently awaiting his esteemed arrival.

"There you are, young man!" Hyatt said. "Now, sit down right there." He ushered Ian to a bench in front of the fireplace, where the other three SOKs were already seated.

"Mr. Hyatt, Mr. Ackerman said to go ahead without him," Ian whispered urgently as Hyatt sat him down.

"Really? That's strange. Anything wrong?"

"No, no. It think it's intestinal. You understand." It was the only excuse he could think of, and it worked.

He took his place next to Curt. Ian prayed for the damn thing to begin so he could disappear into the night air.

"Now, men," Hyatt began, "this is the moment we've all been waiting for . . . the lighting of the first fire in our magnificent new fireplace.

"I'd like to start off by offering these hardworking boys from Deerslayer a round of applause." He urged the others to join him as he clapped his hands in salute.

"I feel like I'm in a goddam lineup," Curt whispered to Ian out of the corner of his mouth.

Freddy and G'Nat beamed.

When the applause died down, Hyatt continued, "And now something a little special. The counselors from the other cabins have prepared a little tribute to you boys. So without any further ado, here they are, the Campettes!" He signaled to the kitchen door, where five counselors were entering in close formation, dressed as extremely top-heavy women in khaki uniforms. The walls of the lodge bulged from the hysterical laughter. As they weaved their mock-feminine way to the front of the room, they jokingly pinched boys and blew kisses, bringing the laughter to an even higher pitch.

Once in chorus line formation, the Campette on the end indicated to Hyatt and said, in a falsetto voice, "Mr. Music Master, if you please!"

On this cue, Hyatt placed a needle on a phonograph and turned up the sound. The scratchy but familiar introduction to "Chattanooga Choo Choo" began, and the Campettes began their well-rehearsed number. They played around the Deerslayers and even Ian had to laugh at their antics.

> Pardon me, boys,
> Is that the crew that built our chimney?
> (Woooo Woo)
> Straight and in line.
> What's more, they finished on time.
>
> They heeded the call
> To be the ones to build our chimney.
> (Woooo Woo)
> Now they're makin' fun.
> Some said it couldn't be done.
>
> You collected all the rockery
> From near and from far.
> You put it all together, men,
> So now here we are.
>
> Nothin' could be finer
> Than to eat in our camp diner,

Dear Deerslayers,
Won't you light our fire?

As they finished the last line, four of them had pulled out kitchen matches from their bountiful blouses and, striking them on the rocks of the fireplace, handed a lit match to each of the Deerslayers.

Taking their cue, the four boys rose, took the matches and, all together, lit the crumpled paper under the bed of kindling and seasoned logs that Ackerman had laid earlier.

The room was silent as the Deerslayers stood back to watch the smoke filter upwards. Before long, the timid flames grew in courage and the kindling became engulfed.

The room filled with cheers.

The fireplace drew perfectly.

When the other boys came forward to thump backs, shake hands, and offer congratulations to the Deerslayers, Ian once again found himself moving away. As the fire began to blaze, he wandered out to the lodge's deck.

Alone, he sat down, pulled the letter from his shirt, and re-read it. He noticed with a smile of curiosity that the letter was written with perfect grammar and spelling, yet oddly, when he read it, he heard Ackerman's Southern drawl.

Ian,

I'm leaving the same way I arrived: secretly and in the night. Up anchor when no one's watching. Easier that way. Don't ask why. Don't look for a reason. Maybe the reason is simply, a reason doesn't exist.

It was you who gave me the idea, you joy riding on ol' Hyatt's boat. You know how I always admired that Chris Craft. They'll find the boat, so it

won't be like stealing. More like borrowing. I got my
sweet Mistress Morphine and a whiskey chaser. When
it's time, I'll ease over the side. I'm a sailor,
remember. I want it this way. No one will know,
except you, son. I reckon, even at the close of things,
no man's an island. Think I'll go see for myself.

I hope I haven't put too much on your
shoulders, Ian. But you're the only one I know
strong enough. And there's room, too, now that
those chips are chiseled down some.

Passing on isn't so bad. It's having nothing to
pass on that hurts. A man has to leave his mark so
the world knows he's been by. So you, Ian
McKenzie, will be my mark. Whatever you become,
so shall I. Whatever you do, so shall I. Whoever you
love, whoever you fight, whatever you think, so shall
I. Maybe that way, some of my dreams are yours and
your dreams mine. So don't go giving up on our
dreams, son. Someday that'll all make sense.
Everything's copacetic here on Fiddlers Green. And
Eeeon . . . don't settle for anything short of paradise.

Andrew Jackson Ackerman

Ian felt burning tears approach, but he damned
them away. He looked out over the cove and saw the red
buoy bobbing in the moonlight where the Chris had
once been moored. He walked into the lodge and shouldered his way through the boys and counselors who were
standing around the fireplace, eating cake and ice cream.
If anyone spoke to him or slapped his back, he was
unaware as he stared into the magnificent fire. He
wadded up Ackerman's letter, tossed it into the eager
flames, and watched as the paper curled up, became consumed, then floated upwards in white ashes in the perfect
draw, the loving embrace, of the chimney.

He left the lodge and slowly walked the waterfront path towards Deerslayer. He could smell the rich aroma of burning wood from the First Fire. He found himself on the dock, exhausted. He sat down, letting his legs dangle over the edge. He leaned back on his hands and looked up into the starry sky.

Ian closed his burning eyes and when he opened them again, they were cleansed. He was lying on the chaise lounge at the end of the dock, breathing in the delicious aromas of a campfire. The songs of the frogs, night birds, and faraway laughter melted together until they were broken by the Bong Bong Bong! of a tennis ball bouncing on the dock and a smiling face of familiar longing.

The admiral sat up, smiled back, tousled the dog's ears, and threw the ball far out into the cove.

twenty-five

Feeling the chill of the night air, McKenzie began walking up the dock, toward land. The last thing his aching body looked forward to was a night in a damp cabin and the confines of a narrow, foreign bed.

Before he could find his way up the path to Deerslayer, the dog had fetched the ball, returned, and shaken off, as though punishing the Admiral for the late night, nautical retrieving. The light from within the cabin cast an uncertain welcome through the small window panes.

As he got undressed and studied the cabin, he slowly began to smile at moonlit memories he was having. So much had been pushed back into a quiet corner of his mind as he had grown older and gained importance in the world. He ventured to speak aloud the names . . . Freddy, G'Nat, Curt.

He stared at himself in the mirror, the cabin light warm, generous, forgiving. The eyes that smiled back were the eyes of his youth, daring — Ian's eyes. He smiled broadly and climbed into bed. Outside his door the dog was begging to be let in. Knowing the animal would probably be as relentless toward gaining entry as he was toward ball-throwing, McKenzie acquiesced, ordering the dog to lie down on the floor, which the dog did, after shaking another layer of the Puget Sound off of himself.

Finally, the admiral's head fell smiling into his pillow as he mentally toasted the memory of the Deerslayers of '44. Even the smell of the wet dog in the small confines of the cabin brought him closer to that summer.

When he walked into the sparkling new dining hall — the Ian L. McKenzie Lodge — the next morning, he felt great . . . greater than he'd felt in months. Although the night's sleep was not his customary 'Admiral's watch,' he found himself refreshed. The smell of burning driftwood mixed with the sweet smell of pancakes and bacon, to intensify his memories. When Canaday greeted him, McKenzie had to fight off the urge to call him Hyatt.

He felt strangely pleased with himself, as though the smug keeper of a wonderful secret. He was out of uniform, without a ship, with no plans beyond a catered speech tomorrow, but he still felt fantastic, hungry, and twenty years younger.

Throughout the day he wandered, with the dog as his guide, from memory to memory. The old, uneven basketball court now offered pickleball and three-walled handball as well; the archery range and the rifle range were worlds safer and better equipped; but the obstacle course, with its tires, ropes, slings, and pitfalls was almost identical. The only new amenity was a fine wooden gate across the path, a mere formality, because any trespasser worth his salt could easily step around it on the trail.

Above the gate, a sign: 'When Gate Is Closed, Obstacle Course Is Off Limits.'

Yeah, sure, McKenzie thought.

There, alone, swinging on a long, heavy rope hanging from a high tree branch, was the skater, Matt Sadler, showing every indication of having been a monkey in a past life. Then, à la Tarzan, he leaped from one rope to another, and dropped down with a quick hop to get his balance.

He caught the rope as it swung back at him and, holding it up to McKenzie, he asked, "Next?"

McKenzie walked toward him and said, "I used to be pretty good on this course."

"What was your time?" Matt asked.

"I don't remember. Let's see how you do. I'll time you." He punched some buttons on his knows-all, does-all watch.

"Okay, but better hang onto that stupid mutt. He'll screw me up."

Delighted to show off, the kid ran to the starting gate and wiped the dust off his hands. He leaned eagerly forward like an Olympic star and waited for McKenzie's order to start.

"Go!" McKenzie called. The dog pulled and barked to be released to set his own record, but McKenzie held him tight.

Matt was amazing. McKenzie wondered how the marvels of nature could evolve such a faster, more agile boy in just two generations.

Matt made it through the course, no slips, no spills, no cheating, in one minute, thirty-six seconds. Barely out of breath, he said, "No one's waxed me yet. But I'm shootin' for a minute, thirty. *No* one's done it faster than that. Ever. How about you? Wanna give it a shot?"

Although he hadn't surrendered to a coughing spasm yet that day, McKenzie knew the obstacle course had to be content with Matt's time.

"What else is there to do around here?" McKenzie finally asked, looking around the woods.

"Polo. But my dossier says I'm not much of a team player. It's a character flaw," Matt replied simply.

"Polo?" McKenzie asked, half believing the punker.

"Did I say polo? I meant baseball. Dude. I'm also a liar."

Baseball. "Is the field still up there?" McKenzie asked Matt, pointing over his shoulder.

"Yeah."

"Come on. I want to look for something."

McKenzie and the boy used field hockey sticks stolen from the well-equipped sports shed to slap through the tall grasses that had, over the years, overtaken the perimeter of the baseball field. According to his recollection, it was just off the third-base line. They scythed their way through the undergrowth like two duffers searching for their golf balls sliced into the wilderness.

"This what you're looking for?" Matt called out, his stick having struck a large stone structure.

McKenzie slashed his way over to him, pulled back the tall grasses, and said, "Yesssss . . . that's it. Here, help me clear around it."

"What is it, a grave?" Matt asked, a little apprehensively.

"That's exactly what it is," McKenzie replied.

"Whose?"

"His name was Kamicurzi, the best damned dog you ever saw." He leaned down and began to brush away the years of undergrowth and dirt. The mutt, delighted with such sport, abandoned his ball and started to dig with his human companions.

"Kami*curzi*? You mean Kamikaze, don't you?"

McKenzie stopped pulling up weeds and replied, smiling, "Well, yes, in a way. But he went by Kamicurzi."

"All this for a dog named Kamicurzi?"

"We worked all night on this dog's grave marker," McKenzie said, leaning back on his heels. "Of course, this was all open ground then." He told Matt the story of the three-legged, suicidal dog. How important he was to a friend of his way back during the war. How the dog had been wounded catching a slug from the muzzle of a rifle, put down in the line of duty.

Matt looked at their dog companion and said, "Scrub. You call yourself a dog? All you ever do is chase this stupid ball."

He threw it, and the dog crashed off into the woods in chase.

They worked for the better part of the morning, clearing and cleaning the area around Kamicurzi's grave. Although it was still well hidden among the grove of trees, the grave itself, should someone wander across it, was respectable once more.

Finally, they'd cleared enough away to read the inscription scrolled into the cement surface of the grave.

"Kamicurzi", McKenzie whispered. "Came and Went

in the Summer of 1944." Odd, he thought. He didn't remember etching any epitaph that night so long ago.

By the time lunch was over, it was clear that Admiral McKenzie and Matt Sadler had adopted each other. McKenzie told Matt stories from his summer at camp and Matt told him stories about the way things were now. So much had changed. So little had stayed the same.

Then they went together to the old lodge. "We can't go in there. That place is condemned," Matt warned as they approached it. "See? Check it out." He pointed to the printed notice on the main entrance: Closed by Order of the Fire Marshal.

"Rank has its privileges," McKenzie said absently, cupping his hands to a window to look inside.

Matt looked at McKenzie, studied him for a moment, and then asked, "Yeah, but does an admiral outrank a fire marshal?"

"Every damn time. Let's go around to the side. There's something I have to see."

Matt followed McKenzie along the side of the lodge. The admiral stopped and looked up at the huge chimney, now completely covered with a thick growth of ivy.

"I never even noticed there was a chimney under all that ivy," Matt said. "You say you helped build this thing? How old were you?"

"Your age," McKenzie replied, tugging away at the base of the structure.

"Sweet," Matt said, obviously impressed. "Now what are you looking for?"

"The cornerstone . . . right. . . " he tugged at the clinging ivy with all his might. When it snapped loose to reveal the mighty stone, he added, ". . . here."

He tugged and pulled some more, this time with Matt's strength behind him, until the stone was completely unveiled.

"It pisses me off they've let it go like this," McKenzie said, pulling at the ivy. "God, we worked hard on it." He stood back, looked up, and noticed that unlike so many other things from the past, the chimney appeared just as high, just as formidable as it had those many years ago.

"Look at that. Ever see a more courageous rock?"

Matt looked at him, gave McKenzie a weak little smile, and said, "Courageous? No way, man. It's been *hiding* here all these years. That rock's a damn coward."

"Nope, son, takes courage to hold all this up. Takes heart," McKenzie said, and then he remembered where he had heard those exact words.

Matt looked at the admiral and smirked, "Takes all kinds."

McKenzie laughed. How well he understood the boy's hesitance. "Come on. Let's go inside."

"I'm cool, but I hope your rank covers me, sailor," Matt said. "Canaday's a real dickwad about rules."

"He can't help himself. It's something inbred into these camp directors. Come on, there's an entrance off the kitchen." When Matt still hesitated, the admiral grinned at him and added, "Trust me."

The old deck well deserved the Fire Marshal's warning, for it creaked and sagged with every cautious footstep. While McKenzie tried to lift the window, Matt wandered in through the kitchen door.

Seeing Matt appear in front of him while he struggled against the stuck window nearly made McKenzie's
heart do a backflip.

"How'd you get in there?" he demanded, almost
hurt that the kid had broken in so fast.

"The door, Ad-mi-ral," Matt chuckled. "The kitchen
door is unlocked."

The inside of the old lodge was as neglected as the
outside. The floorboards moaned at the intrusion, and
the air was musty and dead.

"Cheery joint," Matt observed.

"Oh, but it was once," McKenzie said, absorbed by
the fireplace at the opposite end. They stood looking at
the giant fireplace, long ago declared useless.

"You and some other dudes made that?" Matt asked,
impressed.

"Every damn stone." He broke his stare and began
looking for the rocks he had commemorated with the
names of the SOKs. "Look, Matt, here's Freddy's rock.
You can barely read it, but see? Freddy." From there, he
found G'Nat, and Curt, and lastly his own, now nearly
black under decades of soot.

Again, looking at the monolith, his face grew
somber. "It's so sad," he said, "seeing it so useless, not
doing what it's intended to. . . "

"Too bad they're gonna tear it all down tomorrow,"
Matt said, pumping a sagging section of the planked
flooring.

"What for?" McKenzie demanded. "You mean just
tear it down? All of it?"

Matt looked around them and replied logically,

"What the hell they need this dump for? Hell, according to the old-liners, they haven't used it in years."

"The fireplace and everything?" McKenzie continued, walking again to the enormous structure, reliving the ache in his back, the sting of his blisters, and the swell of pride he'd shared so long ago.

"Hey, you didn't read your brochure. Haven't you noticed that bulldozer out back? It's all part of the ceremony. Out with the old, in with the new bullshit. Symbolism. Hell, Canaday's been telling us that watching this relic fall will be the highlight of our summer."

"I thought it was just going to be a dedication. . . " McKenzie said, running his hands along the mantel, blackened with the soot of ages.

"What, you wouldn't have come if you knew they were pulling this thing down? Looks like Canaday chumped you good," Matt said, a trace of sarcasm in his voice.

"I don't know. . . ," the admiral whispered.

"Look, I don't know about you, but if Canaday finds me here, he'll bust my ass for sure," Matt said, backing away.

Just then, the dog barked at them from behind, startling them both.

"Check it out," Matt said. "Even the damn dog knows we gotta get outa here."

In that startled moment, McKenzie saw flashes of Freddy's sarcastic wit, G'Nat's innocent eyes, Curt's handsome smile, his own cockiness and, of course, Kamicurzi's dead-on warning.

"Yeah, okay. Go on ahead, kid. I'll be out in a minute. See you around."

When he was alone in the once great hall, McKenzie stood back and stared at the fireplace. The idea of a bull-dozer, in one easy tug, pulling down the memories of the best summer of his life made him furious.

He walked to the boarded-up windows which looked out over the cove below. He pulled open the old French doors and stepped out onto the deck. There in the cove was a bright red buoy, bobbing in the gentle current. The greens of the firs, the water, and the hills on the opposite shore brought a painful sting of familiarity. He closed his eyes and he could clearly recall the mysterious emerald of Andy Ackerman's eyes staring down at him as though, once more, goading him onward.

twenty-six

"But why, Mr. Canaday, why are you. . . "

"Please, call me Ted."

"But, Ted, why are you tearing that building down? It must have years of service left. All it needs is some work and. . . " McKenzie tried to keep his voice low and diplomatic at the lunch table, hoping his cool blue eyes expressed his adamant opinion.

"Now, Admiral, that poor old lodge has been in mothballs long enough. Now that we have our beautiful new Ian L. McKenzie Lodge, why keep that eyesore around? It's a fire trap and a danger to the rest of the camp. Surely you can see that. Besides, we need the space for newer and better things, for the new computer center the board is funding. A fine addition to Roswell." Canaday helped himself to a third sandwich. "The kids'll be able to sit, look over the cove, and program the hell out of the Mormons." He laughed over his joke, some bread crumbs escaping as he did so.

McKenzie noticed that the camp director hardly made eye contact at all during his spiel. But, determined not to let it go that easily, he said, "But, Mr. Canaday . . . Ted . . . that beautiful fireplace. All the work it must have taken to build it . . . all gone . . . in one sweep?"

Canaday leaned back in his chair, swallowed, dashed

his napkin efficiently across his lips, and asked, "Don't you care about computer technology, Admiral?"

"Well, certainly, but I don't see what that has to do with preserving a . . . a landmark," McKenzie continued, wishing he'd worn his uniform that day.

"Landmark, schmandmark," Canaday returned, a patronizing smile crossing his face. "That old fireplace didn't even draw a decent fire anymore. Believe me, Admiral, I appreciate your passion, but our engineers have nixed the idea of saving that place. It's only rock and wood, you know. It's not like it's the chapel or anything sacred."

McKenzie, after a lifelong entanglement in red tape, recognized a snafu when he saw one. He excused himself with an apology, saying he hoped his vehemence would not cloud the joy of the following day, but thinking the entire time, Situation Normal: All Fucked Up.

McKenzie spent the remainder of the day piecing together the flood of memories, allowing the sights, sounds, and smells of that summer long ago to penetrate him as he'd never let them before. He leaned back in the chair on the Deerslayer porch, feet up on the railing, rocking back ever so gently, looking out over the cove . . . just like . . .

"Ackerman," he whispered, for the first time speaking the name out loud. The towering pines overhead seemed to nod back as they gently waltzed on the breeze. McKenzie smiled as he realized maybe he'd learned more that summer than how to smoke. Maybe that sailor had influenced him more than he cared to admit. Meybe so, meybe so, he could hear Ackerman drawl. Meybe so.

By dinner, a few more luminaries and ex-campers had checked into camp. They were proudly introduced to the children by Canaday who, McKenzie noted with a hopeless smile, seemed to be gathering momentum by the minute for tomorrow's dedication/destruction festivities.

McKenzie was quiet, but cordial. He much preferred the company of Matt Sadler to the mucky-mucks who, in turn, seemed to not only prefer, but insist upon, his company over any other's. He excused himself during a break in the evening's festivities.

The service access road led him to the back entrance to camp. He recognized the grinding of Matt's skateboard wheels on the pavement long before he saw him. Matt glided by him, hair flying in the breeze. The mutt followed, ball in mouth, happy to run forever thus. The kid saluted and continued on by. Then he stopped, flipped his board up, and said, "Hey, sailor, wanna try?"

McKenzie looked at the kid, still not believing anyone would purposely do that to his hair. "You'd just love to see me try, wouldn't you?"

"Yeah," Matt replied cockily, handing the board out to McKenzie. "Come on, gramps. I'll bet you the thirteen half-finished key lanyards I've started you can't skate to that gate before wiping out." He pointed to the gate at the end of the service road.

McKenzie considered the tradeoff. Suicide for pride? "What the hell would I do with thirteen half-finished key lanyards?" McKenzie asked, feeling a temptation to take the kid up on it.

Matt pulled a jumbled mass of multi-colored plastic

gimp out of a pocket and replied, "Make terrific Christmas presents. Bet the grandkids would love 'em."

"I don't have any grandkids. What else you got?"

Matt frowned as he went through his pockets. "Four dollars worth of camp scrip?"

"No good."

Matt looked around and said, "Hey, dude, I'm just a poor, underprivileged SOK."

"Cry me a river. What else you got?"

"A souvenir stolen from camp."

"Don't need any more silver."

"Something better."

"What?"

"Ah . . . it's a surprise. Hell, I don't know why you're bitchin'. You'll chew it before you get even halfway."

"And what do you want if I do chew it?" McKenzie asked skeptically.

Matt looked dubiously toward the far off gate, then down at his skateboard, and replied, "You'll be fair."

The admiral considered Matt's face under the shock of hair. He had no intentions of telling Matt that, while stationed in the Philippines in the late seventies, he'd held the base skateboarding championship.

"All right . . . dude . . . you got yourself a bet." He took the board and added, "But I'll tell you this; it better be one helluva good surprise."

"Trust me," Matt said, grinning ear to ear.

McKenzie put the board down on the pavement and carefully placed his right foot forward. "You just watch this, punk," he said, lifting his left foot up and settling his weight forward. Only a slight push and he was off, careening down the hill, past the tennis courts and straight on toward the staff parking lot gate. When he reached the gate, he toetapped to a stop, flipped the board up, as he had seen Matt do, and caught it. The run couldn't have been more perfect.

Matt, who had chased after the flying admiral, with the dog barking at his side, screeched to a stop and stood, hands on hips. "Holy shit! Talk about a kamikaze! You can skate with me anytime. Guess I better go snake your surprise."

McKenzie handed the board back, slicked back his thin, wiry hair, and replied, "Nothing too garish, now. Something simple, yet striking." Then, using the kid's vernacular, he added, "Later, bro."

He started walking up the hill, holding back a cough and a smile, wondering how he'd managed to keep his breath and balance. The Philippines and the seventies were a long time ago.

He laughed, starting a coughing spasm, but somehow it didn't matter that day.

twenty-seven

Like so many times in 1944, McKenzie found himself walking in the opposite direction when it was time for evensong. It was the one time, he figured, he could have the camp entirely to himself. Although that evening, the evening before the dedication, he had figured wrong.

The picnic grounds were being prepared for the following day, and Ted Canaday was overseeing the operation. McKenzie stopped short, thankful he saw Canaday before Canaday saw him. McKenzie noted by the chairs being set up below that they were expecting quite a crowd. The new lodge was being decorated with red-white-and-blue bunting, while the old lodge, small and disgraced in its shadow, was cordoned off by plastic tape which warned DO NOT CROSS every three or so feet. Red, of course.

From behind, he heard the chug of large machinery and stepped aside as a bulldozer, decorated with streamers, slowly approached him. The large, clean, shining blade seemed to smile proudly at him as it rolled by. The driver took it to the base of the chimney, where he killed the engine and hopped out.

McKenzie walked to the registration table, saw a box labeled 'Roswell Progs,' and took one out. As Matt had said, part of the ceremony was the destruction of the chimney while the luminaries sat, watched and applauded. This action would be followed immediately by the dedication — his dedication — of the new lodge. Out with the old and in with the new, just like Matt had warned. How tidy.

McKenzie watched Canaday approach the old lodge and stop to talk to the bulldozer driver. He made great sweeping motions with his arms, pointing to the chimney and the chain, which was now wrapped around the chimney's top. McKenzie knew they were orchestrating how the dramatic destruction was to unfold.

The bulldozer driver then got back aboard the vessel, started it up with a chug, turned it around, backed it up close to the base of the chimney, and moved it even closer, as directed by Canaday.

"Great! That's it!" he shouted. "Just perfect! Leave her there and connect that chain to the pull bar or whatever that thingie there is."

The bulldozer wound down and chugged to a halt. The driver hopped down, connected the chain, then walked back toward the machine shed at the service entrance.

McKenzie followed him, keeping well out of his sight. Recalling days of truck stealing and joy rides at the expense of Camp Roswell, McKenzie spied into a window and saw where the dozer key, still swinging back and forth, hung temptingly from a nail.

Stealing the key was as easy as waiting for the driver to leave, entering the shop, and slipping the key off the hook. Atrocious security, he admonished.

Maybe he thought that by stealing the key he could forestall the demolition. Maybe. He had no idea. All he knew was that he whistled all the way back to Deerslayer and that, for the first time in months, he fell asleep without the help of medication.

Then, a short while later, he snapped awake so suddenly, he wondered if he was still alone in the cabin. He lay there awake, trying to recall if he had dreamt the scheme or if inspiration had simply slapped him awake.

He sat up and mumbled to the darkness, "Screw it! I'll tell you what, Canaday. If anyone takes down that chimney, it sure as hell ain't going to be you!"

He got up and began to dress, still mumbling: "So, it doesn't draw anymore, eh? Well, we'll fix that!"

He passed the mirror and caught his ghostly reflection. Then, as clear as though it were yesterday, he heard Ackerman say, "Tear her down an' start all over again. . . "

A smile came to his face. "That's right, tear her down," he replied to the memory.

He looked at his watch. Almost 2400 hours. The best time, as he recalled, for intrigue and reconnaissance. He knew Matt Sadler was the man for this mission. But he had no idea where in the Roswell compound he would find his accomplice. This called for a most desperate, diabolical plan . . . one that would have just popped into his head when he was fifteen and full of master works.

This was a co-ed camp now, he reminded himself, so forget about a cabin-to-cabin search. Records, he told himself. Somewhere in this place they have records of which cabin each kid is assigned to. Simple.

He recalled the tour Canaday had taken him on. The infirmary. Of course. Surely cabin assignments were on file there.

He dressed in his darkest clothes, snatched the bull-dozer key and the flashlight Canaday had so graciously provided him, and left Deerslayer.

It took a moment to get his bearings, but he soon knew he had taken the right path to the infirmary. As he recalled, a nurse was assigned to permanent quarters there, so he knew his mission was risky. He tried not to think of what Canaday or the board might think if he, the meritorious guest speaker, were found going through the camp's medical records. At one point, thinking of the layers of gold leaf that decorated his now retired uniform, he almost turned back. It was stupid, it was downright lunacy, he told himself as he pressed on.

He blessed the new steps up to the infirmary, for they offered him no complaint. The office window was open to the night breezes, and McKenzie felt a little cheated that this might turn out being an easy mission. He carefully climbed in and, flashing his light around the room, looked for files.

"Too easy," he said, shaking his head as he pulled out the file drawer labeled 'Cabin Assignments.' Got to talk to Canaday about security measures, he mumbled to himself, shaking his head.

In the file drawer were alphabetical listings of each camper's pertinent physical and medical information and their cabin assignment.

McKenzie panicked when he realized he had forgotten Matt's last name. Finally, it came to him and he flipped to Sadler. 'Sadler, Matthew, 13, cabin 10. SOK. No allergies. Drug re-hab.' It was difficult not to read on, for the card — the dossier, as Matt called it — could tell him so much more about the boy. But he closed the file drawer, not caring to know anything more. He simply and honestly liked the kid . . . foul mouth, punk haircut, street smarts, and all.

As easily as he had entered, he exited. Even as he was looking for Cabin Ten, he had to laugh at himself . . . 63, retired Rear Admiral, sneaking about camp like . . . well, like a kid, a kid in search of some fun, a kid with major vandalism on his mind.

Cabin Ten, about as far from Deerslayer as one could get, was dark and foreboding. McKenzie studied his next problem: how to get Matt, and only Matt, out.

He looked on the cabin porch, and there, leaning against the wall, was Matt's skateboard. He recalled how Freddy would pop awake when he heard the sound of a marshmallow box being opened. How well Curt could hear the gentle escape of carbonation from a beer bottle. He crept upon the deck, grabbed the skateboard, and slowly ran it over the uneven decking of the porch.

The sound was returned by the sound of a thick canine tail thumping on wood. If understanding certain aspects of human nature was a basis for elevating in rank, McKenzie knew he could have been a full Admiral based on this one, strategically brilliant calculation.

The door opened and Matt, standing only in baggy boxer shorts, peeked out. He looked down and saw McKenzie with his hand on his skateboard. He shut the door behind him and folded his thin arms parentally across his chest. "And just what the hell are you doing? Is this what they teach you in the Navy?" he whispered harshly. "If you want to borrow my board, ask!"

"Come on, kid, we have a job to do," he said urgently. It never occurred to him that Matt might hesitate.

"I don't work past midnight."

"Come on, Matt. I'll tell you about it on the way."

"If I get assed-out for one more thing around here, Canaday'll send me home."

"I'll fence for you."

"Hey, no one takes the heat for Matt Sadler!" he said, for the first time sounding like a true hood rat.

McKenzie stopped and said to him, "Okay. So, you coming?"

Matt looked down at McKenzie, as though weighing the possibilities. "You sure you're not the kind of man my mom's warned me about?" he asked suspiciously.

McKenzie, taken aback by his direct line, gave a ridiculous frown and said, "Don't be stupid. Get your clothes on and meet me at the old lodge," he ordered, flashing the light on the path downward.

"Shit," Matt muttered as McKenzie started to leave.

Although he had been hesitant, Matt showed up within a few minutes, full of excitement and expectation. McKenzie briefed him on their mission. The dog, of course, accompanied him with great joy, anxious for any intrigue. After all, the Humane Society was calling in the morning.

twenty-eight

"**D**ude, are you crazy?" Matt demanded in a high whisper. "That's vandalism! That's worse than vandalism . . . that's . . . that's. . . ."

"Vengeance," the admiral inserted, inspecting the area to assure their privacy.

"I recall somewhere it says vengeance belongs to God," Matt continued, turning to leave.

"You call yourself a SOK?" McKenzie challenged.

Matt stopped, turned, and said, "And I suppose you know how to drive one of those." He pointed to the awaiting bulldozer.

"How hard can it be?"

"Yeah, well I suppose they just left the keys in it, like they *trust* all us happy campers," Matt added.

"Are you kidding? he said, "That would be asking for trouble." At that, he dangled the key in front of Matt.

Matt gave a smiling heave of resignation and said, "Whoomp. Oh, what the hell. They're tearing it down tomorrow anyway."

"That's the spirit," McKenzie said. "Now, we have to work fast. I figure we'll have maybe five minutes tops before Canaday comes running down here."

They worked with the blessing of moonlight. On the

count of three, McKenzie started the bulldozer and prayed that it started easy, without complaint, and didn't resound too loudly through the still of the green night. Then, with Matt at a safe distance and the dog next to him at the controls, McKenzie slowly, gently eased out. The chain grew taut and complained about the strain.

The decaying mortar began to crumble as soon as the chain dug in. With a hesitant thrust of the handles, the bulldozer slipped forward and before he could look behind his shoulder, McKenzie knew the giant edifice was stumbling to its knees . . .

He put the rig in neutral and ran over to Matt. Within seconds, the once grand monolith was a humble pile of rocks at the base of the lodge . . . just as it had started out to be, so many wars ago.

"Nothin' to it," Matt said.

The admiral looked up the side of the building at the scar his handiwork had left. "Come on, kid. We're not done yet."

"What? Why not? You didn't say anything about. . . "

But McKenzie was busy working the chain around the coveted cornerstone. "I'll be goddamed if they're going to haul this away to some landfill!"

He worked like a madman, but secured the chain and quickly scrambled into the cab. Once again, he eased the bulldozer out. The giant cornerstone acquiesced easily and, with Matt guiding him, McKenzie pulled it free and clear of the rest of the rubble.

Matt undid the chains, while McKenzie eased the rig around, lowered the giant blade until it touched the stone, and called for Matt to join him in the cab.

McKenzie drove the bulldozer toward the cliff above

the cove, gently nudging the cornerstone along before it. He brought the rig as close to the edge as he dared. Then he slowly lifted the blade, giving the stone one last, easy push. The great cornerstone slipped forward and crashed down the cliff, rolling victoriously toward the water. McKenzie killed the engine and awaited the sound of the cornerstone reaching its final resting place. When the great stone reached the water, McKenzie smiled over to Matt.

"She always knew where she needed to go. Rest in peace," he whispered mysteriously. "Come on, kid. We better get out of here." The admiral leaped out of the cab and only then noticed how hard he was coughing.

Walking back up toward the old lodge, they stopped to take a last look at their deed. The moon escaped a scrim cloud and reflected light off an object where the cornerstone had so peacefully lain for all those years.

"Hey, what's that?" Matt asked, dropping to his knees and scraping away the dirt.

McKenzie flashed the light on it.

"It's some kind of a box!" Matt said, tugging at it.

"Leave it be, kid. We're on borrowed time." He looked around and saw that the woods around them were alive with the eyes of curious campers. The counselors were talking among themselves, looking around for someone with enough authority to question the activity.

"If I can only get a grip . . . there . . . shit, I lost it!" Matt insisted, tugging furiously at the box.

"Somebody go get Mr. Canaday!" a voice called out from the darkness.

"Oh, for Christ's sake!" McKenzie snapped, pulling

the box out from the rubble with a rough jerk. "Let's get out of here."

"Follow me," Matt said, leading them around to the back of the old lodge. "Ditch that light," he commanded, as though he were the admiral and McKenzie the recruit.

McKenzie tossed the flashlight into the woods and, of course, the dog took chase.

In the dark, Matt led them in and out of the trees and bushes, weaving an intricate, undetectable road to safety. They arrived at Deerslayer the back way. Coming toward them was a bobbing light. Then, to their concerted relief, the dog arrived, carrying the still lit flashlight and obediently depositing it at their feet.

Once safely inside, McKenzie closed the curtains and switched on the lamp.

He placed the box on the desk and began wiping years of damp dirt off of it.

"What is it?" Matt asked.

"It's an old ammo box," McKenzie answered. "General issue during the war. The Second World War." He started to work away at the caked-on dirt until the latch along the top of the metal container was visible.

He pulled up the rusty latch until it finally complied with an unwilling snap. He looked at Matt, handed him the box, and said, "Here. You open it."

Matt opened the ammo box and looked inside. He pulled out a flat black box and carefully opened it.

"Dude, some kind of a medal." He showed it to McKenzie, who put it up to the light.

"A Purple Heart," McKenzie said, a smile slowly coming across his face. He held up the heart-shaped medal. He was barely able to make out the profile of George Washington. "Ackerman's," he whispered.

"Who's Ackerman?" Matt asked, looking back into the box. "Check it out." He held up a black wallet and handed it to McKenzie. The wallet was stuck shut, but McKenzie was able to carefully pull it apart. He gingerly pieced through the contents until he found a folded note. Even after all the years, McKenzie recognized his hand-writing. McKenzie grabbed his glasses from the desk and read aloud:

> What you have found is a kind of time capsule,
> I reckon. Since everything gets torn down some day,
> I've left this here. What's in this box is almost
> everything I have. The one thing I'm taking with me
> is my dignity. I still have that. The rest is yours,
> whoever you may be.
>   *Andrew Jackson Ackerman, August 1944.*

"You knew this dude?" Matt asked, reaching into the box for the last article.

"I guess I did," he muttered, trying to shake himself of the chill passing through him.

"Do you have one of those, too?" Matt asked, not terribly impressed with the Purple Heart.

"No," McKenzie replied, his eyes suddenly fastened on the other box — oblong, black leather, tarnished silver hinges. "Open that one."

Its fastener was difficult to spring open, and while Matt tried to pry it, McKenzie's memory sojourned back to a sleepless night, the summer of '44, in a boat shed with Ackerman and Kamicurzi.

The fastener broke off, and Matt opened the box.

But the green velvet no longer cradled a syringe. In its place was another medal.

Of all the other medals Ackerman could have left, the Congressional Medal of Honor was the last one McKenzie expected to find. He was humbled in the rare honor's simple beauty and grace.

"That's a Medal of Honor, Matt," McKenzie said solemnly, reaching out to pull it from its resting place. Goosebumps raced up his arms and seemed to gather in his throat, forcing him to swallow hard. The blue silk ribbon had rotted some, but the thirteen white stars were still brilliant under the light. His heart ran wildly as he looked at the anchor that attached the five-pointed star to its ribbon.

"So, what do you gotta do to get this one?" Matt asked innocently.

The admiral thought for a moment as he stared respectfully at the gold medal and then replied, "Everything." His voice cracked, bringing Matt's eyes up to his.

"I've never heard of a Medal of Honor before," Matt said, smiling a little, as though to apologize to McKenzie for his ignorance.

"That's because they don't give them out to just anyone." He looked at Matt, his bi-colored hair shining impudently in the gleam of the cabin's faint light. Then his face spread with its own light of discovery. "My God. It . . . was . . . Ackerman. . . "

"Huh?"

"Ackerman appointed me. . . " He turned and looked out the same window he'd stared out so often — stared out at Ackerman rocking, humming his damn "Paradise" on the cabin's porch. "Annapolis. He's the one."

"You lost me, general," Matt said, almost absently.

"Never mind. Doesn't matter. Anyway, a kid your age isn't supposed to know about these things. These are the things of war."

In those seconds that followed the discovery, McKenzie had traveled once around the universe . . . he had returned to the point where he had started . . . full circle: Ackerman to war, peace, death, McKenzie to war, peace, death. Somehow it all made perfect sense. And he'd had the arrogance all those years to think he'd achieved an appointment to Annapolis strictly on intelligence and some long-forgotten math teacher's string-pulling.

He picked up the ammo box and swiped the desk clean, humbled by the smell of the dirt.

Matt got up, carefully returned the medals to their boxes, and handed them to McKenzie.

"No, those are for you," the admiral said, smiling.

Matt looked at him in astonishment. "No, you said you knew this Ackerman guy. Here, I couldn't take 'em."

"No, you found them and risked getting caught for them. Just keep them to yourself. The way Ackerman did. Don't go flashing them around."

McKenzie, feeling suddenly exhausted, sat down on his bunk. He held Ackerman's wallet in his hand.

"Shit, I'd better take off. It'll be just like Canaday to do a cabin-to-cabin bed check to find the SOK that screwed up his ceremony." He closed the two small boxes and smiled down at the admiral. "Hey, you're looking a little tired yourself."

"I guess I am a little beat. Hey, Matt. . . " He stopped at the door. "Thanks. Dooood."

"No big." He held the boxes up, jerked his long bangs back, and said, "I owe you one."

McKenzie looked down at the dog lying peacefully on the floor of Deerslayer. "Take your friend with you," he said as Matt was leaving.

"No way, if Canaday. . . "

"All right, I know the rest. Sure, kid, he can stay here."

Matt smiled and left, carefully latching the door behind him.

twenty-nine

McKenzie knew by the way Ted Canaday glowered at him at breakfast the next morning that he knew he'd had something to do with the chimney's premature demise. Although he hadn't the nerve to accuse the admiral, their exchanged glances left little to the imagination. Canaday worked little hinty phrases like 'role model,' 'shining example,' and 'positive influence' into the light conversation. McKenzie nodded, looked thoughtful, stared coolly back at Canaday.

Fortunately, with the steady arrival of the guests, the parents, the alums, the etcetera that patronize events such as dedications and reunions, there was little time for McKenzie and Canaday to discuss the matter any further.

By ten, McKenzie was putting on, perhaps for the last time, his dress whites. He arranged the various legions of pins, braid, medals, and decorations with second-nature expertise. Then, recalling that the Humane Society would be looking for the mutt, McKenzie latched the Deerslayer door on the protesting dog. He stood on the porch, listening to the dog's whine on the other side of the door, and then, a half hour late, headed to the festivities down by the new Ian L. McKenzie Lodge.

Matt was nowhere to be seen, and McKenzie wasn't surprised. No doubt Canaday had sent him out on an expedition far and safely away from the pristine ceremonies about to unfold.

So McKenzie found himself, once again, glittering white on a speaker's platform, sitting in the sun, and awaiting his turn to speak. Canaday, in his ill-fitting city suit and his best center-stage form, was the first to speak after the invocation.

"You know," he began, a hand plunging into a pocket in order to appear more casual, more camp-like, "it's not every day a Roswell camper returns to us after an absence of nearly fifty years. It's not often we send out a tired camper into a world at war and get back a Rear Admiral, either. You have only to glance at the hardware on his chest to see his exceptional service record. But Admiral McKenzie brings to us more than that; he brings to us the essence of our very Roswell motto: Physical Strength, Moral Courage, and Mental Fortitude. So now, campers, parents, and esteemed friends, I present to you Rear Admiral Ian L. McKenzie, United States Navy, Retired."

There was applause as McKenzie took the podium. Although he smiled toward the crowd, he didn't even look at Canaday as he passed him. "Thank you, Mr. Canaday, for those heartfelt words," he began. Then he took a few pages of typed, generic speech out of his pocket, cleared his throat, and held the pages up to the audience.

"One of the advantages of being in the upper echelons is that you have an adjutant, an aide to help you. One of my aide's last official duties for me was to write this speech. Two days ago I would have read this to you, you would have clapped politely, and an hour later none of us would have remembered a word. So I think I'll save this for another day."

He folded the paper up and replaced it in his coat pocket. He looked out over the crowd, then at the serene beauty of the cove beyond.

"Since returning to Camp Roswell, I've had a very interesting retrospection . . . which, I suppose, is what returning, coming back, is for. But memories of the past mean nothing until you put them to good use in the here and now. Also, the here and now means nothing unless you provide for tomorrow. I call this the natural order of things."

He ventured an ever-so-slight glance back toward Canaday and continued. "As you can see by reading your program, Camp Roswell's tomorrows are well provided for. Knowing this wonderful new lodge will provide fine times, great memories, for generations of future campers, I find myself having to abdicate the honor of having the lodge dedicated in my name."

There was a slight breeze and, with it, some uncomfortable rustlings from the audience. Although he kept his gaze out front and direct, he was sure Canaday was now sitting straighter, getting redder.

"For you see, I'm not the most notable or worthy Roswell camper on the past rosters. My name is not the name I would like to be remembered here. The name we all need to remember is Andrew Jackson Ackerman. Compared to this one man, I'm really quite ordinary and my accomplishments pale in comparison."

Now there were slight whisperings in the crowd, and McKenzie paused, took a drink of water, and now looked slyly around at Canaday, who was sitting in his chair as straight as an oar, glaring at him.

"So who was Andrew Jackson Ackerman? Just a sailor, a Seaman, First Class who passed into obscurity almost fifty years ago. Just a sailor. Yet, looking back, I realize he was the most troublesome, challenging, and influential person in my life. You see, sometimes we are more than just ourselves — a person is the work of many and we carry with us the hopes and dreams of others. Somewhere along the line, there is a primary influence." He paused. "Ackerman was mine."

He scanned the crowd for Matt, but saw only faces of gentle confusion, absent-minded respect, and a few sweet smiles.

"So, rather than accept this honor, I would like to, in its place, announce a college scholarship fund I am going to establish. It doesn't matter to me what you call it, but, starting next year, I will endow this scholarship. . . "

The crowd wanted to applaud, but McKenzie kept talking louder to be heard above them. "This scholarship will go to what we call an SOK — Service Organization Kid, for those of you who don't know. I will ask for only three qualifications for this SOK candidate: promise, initiative, and courage."

He finally allowed the enthusiastic round of applause. When it died down, he finished, "That expressed, I would like to thank you once again for the honor you've given me and for indulging me this one executive privilege of passing this dedication honor on to one far more deserving. Ladies and gentlemen and campers, it is my extreme good fortune to present to you the Andrew Jackson Ackerman Lodge." He gestured toward the lodge, now proud in its red-white-and-blue adornment. The fine new cedar sparkled in the sun, the decks stuck out proudly, the windows smiled back the reflection of those gathered next to it.

The applause seemed genuine, if not a little confused. He turned the podium back to Canaday and, with little encouragement from his lungs, he was taken over by a coughing spasm so severe, he conveniently excused himself from the rest of the ceremony.

Feeling exhausted, feeling vindicated, and feeling the need to get on with his life, he arranged to be picked up that afternoon. Nothing was left for him at Camp Roswell now.

He excused himself from the remainder of the activity-crammed day. Canaday was an odd amalgam of 'how dare you!' and 'how wonderful!'

As McKenzie started to walk the path back up to Deerslayer to collect his grip, Canaday followed him, "But, Admiral, there are so many details to work out. About your wonderful and generous scholarship program."

McKenzie kept walking and said, "I'll have someone get in touch with you."

"But, Admiral, if we are to administer it, why there's *tons* of paperwork to fill out," he gushed, keeping pace.

McKenzie turned, smiled vaguely, then asked, "Got a piece of paper?"

Naturally, Canaday had a note pad and pen in one of his pockets. He gave them to McKenzie.

McKenzie scribbled two words, then handed the pad back to Canaday. "Here. Here's all you need for now."

He turned and started back up the path, wondering

if that was the mutt's lemme-me-outa-here yelps coming from Deerslayer he heard in the distance.

Canaday looked at the paper and hollered, "Matt Sadler? You want that bas. . . that *punker* . . . Matt *Sadler?*"

McKenzie climbed the steps to Deerslayer for the last time and released Mutt by throwing the tennis ball far down the hill. He smiled as he heard the ball hit the water, followed by the belly-flop splash the dog made in wild chase. He rubbed his shoulder, packed his grip, and took one last, loving look around the cabin, as though to seal it forever in his memory.

Matt was still absent. It would have been just like Canaday to have confined him to quarters in retaliation for all of McKenzie's little treasons, insults, and incendiaries at his expense. But it was just as well, he told himself, just as well Matt had disappeared — he would have himself, back in forty-four, and he was about to once again. Matt was going to be all right. Besides, good-byes were getting to be more and more difficult.

He waited by the entrance for his ride back to Bremerton. Alone again in the woods, he looked up at the tree tops and allowed himself to become mesmerized by their sway, their whisper, their stories of the past.

When Lt. Harding arrived and got out of the car, McKenzie found himself tired and anxious to return to the base to finish his packing and see what brochures had arrived from Arizona.

"Did you have a good time, sir?" the lieutenant asked.

"Yes, as a matter of fact, I had a great time."

Lt. Harding looked down the trail beyond the admiral and said, "I see you found yourself a new recruit."

McKenzie looked around and saw that the dog had silently emerged from the forest, patiently sitting behind him, dripping wet, leggings of sand and mud, ball in frothy mouth.

"Him? He's a pest and a fanatic," he said, giving the dog a final pat.

Lt. Harding picked up the admiral's grip and headed toward the car. But McKenzie hesitated.

"Forget something, sir?"

He looked at the dog, who dropped the ball, then barked insistently. He tossed the ball far into the woods beyond, and waited for the dog to dive into the underbrush. "Go get it, Mutt!" But this time the dog didn't budge, only sat and wagged his tail as though to suggest the man retrieve his own damn ball this time. "Okay, so don't go get it," McKenzie said down to the dripping creature. "Come on, Lance, I'm ready."

McKenzie got in the back seat. While the lieutenant was putting the grip into the truck, McKenzie noticed a slight bulge in his canvas briefcase. He reached in and his hands felt cool, hard objects. Inside the case were four small stones. He pulled them out, and a huge grin graced his face. They were the signature rocks from the fireplace, and wrapped around Curt's rock, with various colored plastic lanyards, a note. In barely legible handwriting, it read,

Hears your dam camp suvineers. Now we're even. Good luck, dooood. Drop me a line if you need skateboard lessins. Matt Sadler, SOK First Class

P.S. Nice speech. Canaday must have shit in his pants.

How Matt had gotten the rocks into his pack would
be eternity's secret. One extraordinary SOK, he thought
to himself as he smiled down at the note — one extraordinary SOK.

His smile grew into laughter and his laughter grew
into coughing spasms. Lt. Harding had closed the trunk,
come around, climbed in. McKenzie was looking into the
sideview mirror. He saw the dog, still sitting, still waiting. The lieutenant slipped the car forward and watched
the admiral as he kept staring in the mirror at the dog,
growing smaller in the distance.

Then, passing them into camp, the truck from the
Humane Society.

The Admiral finally touched Lt. Harding lightly on
the shoulder and gave him the signal to stop. The back
door opened and the woods echoed back the admiral's
shrill whistle. The dog sprang forward, ran toward the
car, and leaped in. The door closed, and the car continued out of the parking lot.

McKenzie closed his eyes, rocks in one hand, the other
hand caressing the camp Mutt, and he thought of the
SOKs of '44.

He never found out what had become of any of
them . . . Freddy, G'Nat, Curt. It was just as well, he
told himself before allowing the warmth of the sun on
his back, the warmth of the dog at his side, to lull him
to sleep. For in his memory they were all better off as
troublesome, mouthy SOKs thrown together in a cabin
called Deerslayer, under the supervision and inspiration of
Andrew Jackson Ackerman.